The Guardian

Eleven Science Fiction Short Stories

edited by Alasdair Shaw

First published 2017
ISBN10 0995511063
ISBN13 978-0995511064

Contents

Introduction

This is the third book in the Scifi Anthologies series that started with **The Newcomer**. As ever, I have had the privilege to choose a collection of great stories from both new and established authors.

Every story in this anthology has a guardian as a central character. Some look after individual people, others whole planets or universes, but all share a strong belief in their responsibility to protect their charges.

#

Algernon Wade and the crew of the *Hansard* arrive to study an abandoned colony for the Exploration Service. They find a highly advanced civilisation that met a grisly end. Their presence triggers an "Awakening".

Rob Treutlen lives in a cage, just like everyone else on Earth. The Reptilian Empire constructed "The Lattice" around the planet, and they persistently demand more work from their captives. Rob hates it, but he has an ailing father to care for, and he can't afford to get involved with the resistance.

His father's death changes that. He seeks out the resistance and attempts to escape. It's dangerous, and his probability of success is low, but he's willing to risk it. Because having nothing left to live for makes some things worth dying for.

They say curiosity kills the cat, but what about a pup with only one life?
What starts out as a desire to see the great unknown outside the den quickly turns into more than "Biting Shadow" ever anticipated when he comes across a dying stranger who is desperately trying to pass on a 'gift'. Now, as an unwitting host to alien technology, Biting Shadow struggles to make sense of the rapid changes made to his biology while also dealing with a hostile presence. These alterations may be the key to saving his family and even the planet, but at what cost to himself?

Andre Damiani is obsessed with finding the lost secrets of the Predecessors, thinking it will bring meaning and fulfilment to his life. When he finds the key to not just his own purpose but that of all life in the universe in a long-lost cache of ancient alien technology, he also finds it threatened by the same Corporate Council masters he's served for decades. Damiani is forced to decide how much he's willing to sacrifice to preserve the "Gate of Dreams" from the greed of men.

A lonely boy walks the empty corridors of a starship with only his dog for company. He guards a precious cargo: one that holds many secrets, one that only he can protect. But when "The Following Star" begins to catch the ship, he soon learns that his whole life has been a lie.

Arlen's a trader, not a scientist. She never expected to be in a first-contact situation.
When an alien species needs her help, she discovers that there are people in the universe like nothing she ever dreamed. People who find her as unique and fascinating as she finds them. People who need her help with "The Renewal".
Sometimes profit isn't everything.

A month ago, Ada Xander had a home, a family, and a normal life working the family mine on Cyron-2. Now she's a "Stowaway", sleeping standing up crammed in a smuggling cabinet on-board a pirate ship.

To survive, she'll need to forge alliances, prove her worth, and become one of the crew. And all that assumes they won't just space her outright if they find her.

Cadet Anjali Patel had hoped for something more exciting than guard duty for her first mission with the legendary Shakyri Expeditionary Corps, the best fighters in the Empire of Worlds. However, this boring job quickly turns hot, when an enemy convoy comes up the mountain pass Anjali is supposed to guard. Her "Baptism of Fire" is more than she bargained for.

When a crew of desperate pirates sets down on a distant frontier world, the only thing between them and an easy payday is one old woman working the fields. But things are often not what they seem. What that woman knows makes all the difference between life and death, and a "Sleeping Giant" is stirring.

It is a foggy night in an alternate Victorian London. Eleanor, a world-famous inventor, fulfills a decades-old pact. In "We Have the Stars", three friends meet, and the revelation that follows shatters Eleanor's perspective on humanity and herself.

A damaged warship can't remember much beyond its mission to defend the planet it orbits. When the *Behemoth* turns up and starts landing its passengers, no-one spots the "Warning Signs".

#

And so, on to the stories. I hope you enjoy...

-o-

Awakening

by Alasdair Shaw

The *Hansard* edged deeper into the unsurveyed system. Main drives powered down, it followed a ballistic trajectory which stretched from its jump point towards the inner planets.

"The computer's identified three jump points and added them to the charts, Algey." Lieutenant Commander Charlotta Delgardo shrugged and rubbed her shoulder. "Looks like we've got the place to ourselves. The only power signatures I can detect are the star and a few volcanoes scattered around the system."

Captain Algernon Wade nodded. "As usual. Guess we ought to start cataloguing. You ready for an active scan, Lottie?"

"Ready as I can be. You know what the *Han's* like."

Algey winced at the insult to his ship, but quickly relaxed when he remembered who he was talking to. "Yeah. Yeah, I do… How's the shoulder, by the way?"

Lottie smiled. "It'll be fine as long as I don't have to do any more heavy lifting for a while."

"Sorry." Algey shrugged and gave a rueful smile back. "You're the best we have at doing those repairs."

"Cheers." Lottie tapped at her console, the blue glare from the screen contrasting with the drab orange decor of the bridge. "Sending first pulse now."

A tinny ping sounded from the speakers, a sad mockery of the alerts when Algey had commanded military vessels.

"Ten minutes 'til we get the first results back. Have you spoken to Mariett today?"

Algey took a deep breath and looked around the empty seats. "No. Is he ready to apologise?"

"He doesn't think there's anything to apologise for."

"He was drunk on duty."

Lottie stretched her legs out in front of her and arched her back. "The way he tells it, he'd knocked off duty and had a couple of drinks before being dragged back for another shift."

"Hmm. That's no excuse. He's our primary helm. He should always be ready."

Lottie glared at him. "Are we really going over this again? This isn't the Navy, Algey. We've gotta give them some slack. The Exploration Service allows alcohol aboard its ships. It's not like we have to stand ready to repel ships trying to intrude on our space."

Algey groaned softly. Had Lottie found out about the Battle of Swan-III? He'd only been a lieutenant on a destroyer back then, the raiding party had caught their squadron off-guard. He'd been at a party at an illegal still when battle-stations sounded and the XO had given him a severe dressing down when he rolled up to his station. He'd been dry ever since. These young-uns needed to learn the lesson too. "OK. Put him back on the rota."

The two sat in silence for a few minutes. Ever since the Republic had fallen into civil war a couple of decades ago, the Indiran Co-operative had prioritised defence in every budget. The Exploration Service, once treated to the cream of the crop, had to make do with a handful of antiquated ships.

Algey picked at the frayed stitching on the arm of his chair. "My money's on another barren system."

"Really? I've got a good feeling about this one." An internal call chimed. "Hello, Doctor Oak. What can I do for you?"

"I was wondering if you had any results for me yet?"

"Sorry, Doc. Another couple of minutes before the return from the nearest planet arrives."

"OK. Keep me informed." A beep signalled the connection was closed from the far end.

"Oh, I will," said Lottie, rolling her eyes. Then she appeared to notice Algey watching her and laughed. "I like Max. Really, I do. He just gets so focussed on his research."

Algey busied himself reviewing the logs from the previous shift. As usual, nothing interspersed with trivia. The most interesting entry was an untraced fault in one of the waste recycling systems. He couldn't send Lottie in again; Mariett perhaps?

"Here we go." Lottie bent over her console, hands dancing across the screen. Her eyes narrowed and her mouth hung slightly open as the tempo increased.

Algey shuffled forward in his seat. "What've you got?"

"Not sure yet." Another pathetic ping announced an active sensor transmission. "Could be nothing, but I've initiated a full-spectrum scan of the planet just in case."

"What do you think it might be, though?" Algey hadn't realised quite how desperate he was to find something noteworthy before the end of the cruise. Anything that might secure his position against the next round of cuts.

"It looked like a near-orbit cloud."

Algey's heart thudded. "Artificial satellites? That's..."

"Don't get excited yet. Wait for the detailed scan."

The comms panel chimed and Doctor Oak's excited voice carried across the bridge. "Are you sure about the data you just sent me?"

Lottie winked at Algey. "The data's good, and I'm sure you came up with the same theory I did, but I don't think it's conclusive."

"We must investigate further," said Oak. "This could be enormous."

"I've already initiated a detailed scan. You'll have the results as soon as they're available."

"Captain, I trust you've altered course to visit this planet?"

Algey managed not to snort audibly. "If the second scan yields positive results, I will certainly divert."

Oak spluttered. "We cannot delay. If this is an ancient colony, we must spend every possible moment investigating it."

"Ten minutes won't make any difference. Changing course, only to have to correct again if the scan results are negative, will waste fuel and reduce our options later on."

"But..."

"Wait for the results, Doc," Lottie said with a smile, then cut the connection. "He'll be waking everyone up. Bet he's nearly bouncing off the ceiling."

"He'd better not disturb Joe and Ed."

Lottie snorted. "He was working in the Service long before you or I transferred from the Navy. He knows better than to rouse anyone on a down-shift."

Butterflies multiplied in Algey's stomach as the minutes passed. A big find might help reverse the decline in the Service. It could be presented to parliament as evidence of their success. A major expedition could be mounted, and the *Hansard* would be in prime position to lead it.

He looked up when Lottie's console lit up with new data. "Well?"

Lottie cycled through her displays before looking up. "The distribution of orbits is too great to be natural, there's everything from polar to geostationary, even retrograde. I can't think what else it could be other than a satellite network."

Algey brought up the nav controls on his console, typed in a set of course corrections, and sent them across to Lottie to check. When she agreed with the calculations, he fed them into the helm control and activated them. The *Hansard* slewed about two axes so its main engines pointed across and slightly up from its current trajectory. The engines powered up, sending a reassuringly steady thrumming through the ship. A minute later, the nav computer piled on the power and the engine thrust pressed Algey into his seat. Seventy-eight seconds of extra weight, then they cut off. Algey checked the new course and nodded to himself, satisfied they were lined up for high-orbit insertion.

#

The shuttle bounced in the turbulent upper atmosphere. Algey held on to the restraints on his seat and studied Dr Oak. The older man seemed oblivious to the violent motion of the craft, focussing on his data pad.

"What do you think, Max?" asked Algey.

The doctor looked up and blinked. "Looks like a highly-developed colony, probably pre-Exodus. It's hard to make a guess at population density when it was occupied, but given the number and size of the cities, I'd put the population in the four to five billion range. Certainly bordering on Core World status."

"They looked pretty intact from orbit. No signs of bombardment." Algey glanced along the row of archaeologists facing him on the other side of the compartment. "Any clues as to why it was abandoned?"

Max shook his head. "You Navy types are so impatient, Algernon. I've not even set foot on the surface and you want answers."

Algey bridled, almost reminding Max about his urgent demand to alter course. A couple of the security team members to his right shifted in their seats, presumably feeling included in Max's accusation.

The shuttle settled into a more smooth flight. Algey took a deep breath, pushing away his annoyance at the lead archaeologist. Being able to come on away missions like this was the biggest perk of commanding an Exploration Service ship instead of a Navy vessel and he didn't want to waste it by getting bogged down in an argument.

"Boss," called the pilot, his voice carrying through the open hatchway between the cockpit and the hold. "The *Han* confirms they've got us and have given clearance to land in the city."

"Thanks," Algey called back. "Did Lottie mention anything about the satellites?"

"She'll send the data to your pad when she's finished."

"OK." Algey drew his sidearm, checked it, and re-holstered it. The security team busied themselves readying their weapons.

Max glared at them then narrowed his eyes and pointedly looked down at his pad. Algey gave thanks that at least he wasn't going to bring up his notion that the security team were just playing at being soldiers. The Exploration Service mandated an armed presence on all missions until such time as a complete absence of threat had been ascertained, and that was all there was to say about the matter. Most of the time, they only had to deal with fauna or the occasional aggressive flora, but from time to time they ran into raiders or people who didn't want to be disturbed.

The shuttle broke through the cloud layer and the pilot brought them in a wide circle around the cluster of skyscrapers that marked the centre of the city. Everyone craned to see out of the windows, the petty sparring lost in the shared awe of setting eyes on a lost civilisation.

The shocking colours of the tall buildings affronted Algey's sense of style, but there was no arguing that they were cheerful. Each tower seemed to vie with its neighbours to sport the most gaudy display; here flowers, there starships, no surface was left without a colourful coating.

"Bring us down there." Max pointed at a small open space on the map displayed on his pad.

Algey looked carefully. "That's not where you said in planning."

"The orbital scans only gave us the layout. I made an educated guess based on cities I've studied before. But look at that building at the north end of the piazza."

Algey peered through the window. "The small, grey one? Oh, I get it." He called through to the pilot. "Land at the coordinates Doctor Oak's sending through to you."

Max tapped on his pad and flicked a finger across the screen towards the cockpit. "Thank you, Algernon."

The shuttle touched down gently, the pilot allowing the engines to unwind into a quiet whirr. "Atmosphere breathable. No sign of pollutants or bio-hazards."

Two of the security team stood and glanced around the compartment, checking everyone was ready, before triggering the side hatch to open. Even before it finished moving, they were out, scanning their weapons from doorway to window to crumbling hole.

Max looked to Algey. "Is this stric..."

Algey raised a finger.

"Clear," came the call from outside. The rest of the security team exited.

"After you, Max." Algey waved his arm to the door with a half-bow. The research team piled out and stood staring around. For once, he shared their wonder. Treading in the footsteps of a lost civilisation.

"OK, you three secure the shuttle." Algey indicated some of the security team. "The rest of you, clear the grey building."

He studied their first target. A flight of stone steps led up to a colonnaded facade, hidden from the elements by a large overhanging roof. After a few moments soaking in the view, he followed the rest of the team inside.

A grand hall awaited him, dust kicked up by the feet ahead swirling in shafts of daylight that slanted across the space. High above him, a small bird fluttered between domed alcoves.

Max was already behind the raised desk in the centre, drawn no doubt by the 'Information' sign hanging above it. Algey mused on how little this colony's language had drifted from Standard during their isolation. He took a seat at one of the hundred or so tables scattered around the room and leant back, studying the intricate designs gilded onto the ceiling.

"Can I get a power source over here?" asked Max.

One of the researchers strode over, slipped a rucksack of their shoulder and pulled out a charge pack. "Reckon one of the standard connectors'll fit? Or will we have to fabricate one?"

"The terminal looks fairly standard, so..." He disappeared under the desk. "Drat, no such luck. OK, let's try splicing into their lead."

Without a standard connector, they'd be a while working out what voltage, current and frequency to use. Algey detailed the security operators to pair off with researchers and explore the surrounding streets. He checked his pad and found an initial report from Lottie. It detailed a fairly standard orbital cloud for a large civilisation. One object many times the size of the *Han*, probably a space station, sat in medium orbit; they were about to focus on scanning it.

#

Algey ran his fingers along the smooth, cold wall, examining the polished stonework for signs of fossils. Before he'd joined the Navy, he'd studied palaeontology, which was probably why the Exploration Service had agreed to take him after the Navy let him go.

A call came over the radio. "Boss? You've gotta see this."

Algey checked his pad, the caller was a security operative two streets away. "What is it?"

"Skeletons, boss. Lots of skeletons."

"On my way." He beckoned Max over. "Looks like we may have found some of the former inhabitants."

Max muttered a few words to the researcher beside him, passing him the scanner he was holding, and trotted over. Algey called one of the security operatives in from the shuttle to stay with the researcher while he continued to attempt to get the terminal working.

Max and Algey hurried to the building they'd been called to. They were directed to a room deep within. As they left the reach of daylight, they flicked on their chest- and head-torches.

A door stood ajar, propped open with a plastic chair. "In here," called someone from inside.

They entered, and stopped dead. A researcher crouched in about the only part of the room not covered in human bones. "They're mostly articulated, though there are signs of peri-mortem dismemberment. From the arrangement, I'd say they died here."

Algey noted the bones pushed to the side by the opened door. This wasn't a mortuary. "They were locked in this room?"

The researcher nodded. She continued to examine the bones.

"We had to break our way in," said the security operative. "It was bolted from the inside."

Algey raised an eyebow.

"What made you try this room?" asked Max.

The operative shone a light on the door. Daubed across it in orange paint was a single word: Help.

"Look here." The researcher held up a femur in her purple-gloved hand, pointing at some scratches near the end. "Knife-marks, I think."

Max picked his way over to her and took the bone. "Indeed. Consistent with butchering, I'd say."

Algey's eyes widened. "They ate each other?"

"Probably. I'd guess the first ones to go were used to keep the survivors alive a bit longer. See how many of the bones are neatly stacked against the far wall? There were still people alive to do that."

"How long did it take?"

"I can't tell." The researcher waved a hand towards one corner of the room. "There's a sink and toilet behind that screen, so they'd have had water. They had rations with them too, at least at the start. About a month's worth, judging by the foil wrappers."

Algey shuddered. "What scared them?"

The researcher shook her head. "Don't know. Presumably whatever brought about the end of their civilisation, or someone would have found them already."

"I take it you'll want to run a full set of tests on these bones, Max?" Algey frowned. "Hang on. Where are their clothes? They can't be more than a couple of hundred years old."

Max smiled. "Assuming they used fabrics like we do. If they wore garments fashioned out of natural fibres, they could easily have decomposed by now."

Algey checked the time. Just over an hour since touch-down and no signs of anything threatening. "OK. I'm calling down another shuttle with a mobile lab. Let's set up base in the grey building."

Algey's radio crackled into life. "Boss, Emma here. We found a hospital. It's carnage. Looks like they were treating people in the corridors, restrooms, anywhere they could cram them in."

Max caught Algey's gaze. "Are you sure there were no pathogens in the air sample?"

"Quite sure, Max... But..." He thumbed his radio. "Listen up, everyone. Just to be on the safe side, I'm ordering level 2 biohazard precautions. Suit and mask up. We'll run everyone through the lab when it gets here."

#

Algey gazed at a towering purple building. Pink swirls defied the eye, appearing to move as he shifted focus from one place to another. Yet again, he wondered how a society could bombard its citizens with such a brash assault on their vision.

A researcher crouched over his rucksack. "I'll need a couple of minutes here to get some readings, then we can move on."

"OK, James. Whatever you need." Algey looked across to the security operator where she stood on a bench, eyes focussed in the distance. Mary was one of the best in the team, a timed-out Marine who'd joined the Exploration Service to continue to protect the Indiran Co-operative's interests.

The dry air tickled his throat and he rummaged through his pockets to find a sweet. He popped one in and sucked, relishing the sticky tang.

"How's it going down there?" Lottie's voice had that faint edge of someone who is really excited about something but knows there's something more pressing to deal with.

"We're fine. They identified a virus in the bones. It's not something we've encountered before, but it has similarities to rabies.

They assure me our standard anti-virals will prevent us getting infected." Algey scratched his neck. "Obviously, we'll have to be careful with decontamination when we leave; don't want to carry it to a planetary population."

Not for the first time, he gave thanks that everyone serving aboard Navy or Service ships was subjected to regular broad-spectrum inoculations.

"We've completed our initial scans of the space-station. Only it isn't." Glee slipped into Lottie's voice. "It's a ship."

Algey stopped walking. "You sure? It's massive."

"We identified drive systems large enough to accelerate it at sizeable G."

His mouth dropped open. Even without calculation, he knew that the power generation systems must have been immense. "Any indication of age?"

"Everything we've examined, including the ship, shares common construction features and metallurgy." Lottie took a breath. "I'd say we're looking at a snapshot of this colony in its last days, but we'd have to snag a sample and analyse the radiation degradation to get a date."

"Go for it. You might have better luck interfacing with a computer than we are, too."

"Any preferences? There's a good range... Something's happening. Wait one."

Algey began pacing. He'd got complacent and was stuck on the planet relying on second-hand information. Captains shouldn't go on away missions.

"OK." Lottie's voice remained calm. "We've got a power source on the native ship. Definitely wasn't there a minute ago."

"Maybe the scans triggered a wake-up sequence?" Algey's heart leapt with excitement. "Get a team ready to go aboard. If it's got power, it might have working terminals, a database."

"Will do. Mariett can lead it."

"No." Algey shook his head. "He's not up to it."

"Well, it's either that, or I go and leave him in command of the *Han*..."

Algey opened his mouth to suggest he came back up and swapped with Mariett, but it would only shift the problem down to the planet. "Fine. But make sure to have a quiet word with the lead security operative before they depart."

He opened up the reconstruction of the ship on his pad. A prolate ellipsoid over two kilometres from tip to tail. The surface was unusually smooth, devoid of the normal clutter of sensors, weapons and heat dumps.

A klaxon sounded over the channel to the *Hansard*. Lottie's voice came back with a hint of awe. "It's locked an active sensor on us. Engines coming online... It's moving!"

Algey's heart raced. Adrenaline pumped through his veins. "How? Sleeper crew?"

"Or AI. I don't know," said Lottie. "It's coming straight for us. The acceleration's phenomenal."

"You got the *Han* running hot?"

"Of course." Lottie called something to someone on the bridge. "Hatches opening across its surface... Looks like weapons ports."

"Run!"

"Ahead of you on that one." Lottie's voice bore the strain of high-G. "It's launching missiles... Correction, single missile."

"Activate CIWS but don't deploy main weapons."

"Not my first rodeo, Algey."

"Sorry." He looked down to see why his hand hurt and found he'd dug his nails into his palm. "Just frustrated at being stuck down here."

"Missile's gone ballistic... It's not tracking with us. Looks like its target is... Algey, take cover, its heading for your position. ETA ten minutes."

Algey's hand went to his radio and pressed the emergency broadcast button. "Everyone, we have incoming. If you're within five minutes of a shuttle, get in and take off. Otherwise find somewhere deep to take cover."

He looked to the security operative next to him. "What do you reckon?"

Mary shook her head. "Seven minute run at best, given the debris."

"Yeah, thought as much. I'm not holding a shuttle that long." He bit his lip. There wasn't anywhere closer for a shuttle to put down to collect them, either. "Let's find some shelter."

They hurried to the nearest building. Mary took the lead, with Algey helping the researcher with his equipment. "How's it going up there, Lottie?"

"The ship's slowing down. It's still maintaining a lock on us, but it seems to be more interested in positioning itself between us and the planet than pursuing."

"Don't hang around." Algey transmitted the data they'd collected on the surface. "Get out of here and bring help."

"Understood, boss. I estimate a couple of hours and it won't be able to catch us before we can jump. I'll deploy a probe so you'll still have eyes in the sky. Good luck down there."

"Over here!" Mary waved from an open doorway.

As Algey and James reached her, the whine of a shuttle taking off carried down the narrow street. They piled inside and followed the operator down a flight of stairs. Then another one. The comms signals from outside cut out.

Three flights later, they came to the plant room for the building. Algey checked the countdown on his pad, which showed a couple of minutes left, and pointed to a gap between large, heavy-looking pieces of equipment. "In there. Ought to give us some protection."

The three of them curled up on the floor, heads in their arms, mouths open to equalise any pressure differences from a shockwave. Algey's thoughts strayed back over his career. At least if this was the end then he was going out on a high.

#

The pad counted through zero and started on negative numbers. Ten minutes had only been an estimate, though, so Algey kept his head down. He ran over and over the damage control and rescue exercises he'd been put through in the Navy, working out what they might have to do to get out of the basement after the strike.

At minus two minutes, however, he began to fidget. Lottie couldn't have been that far out. Perhaps the ordnance had been so degraded with age it'd broken up in the atmosphere? A glance at the other two people sharing the shelter showed they must be having similar thoughts; James even had his head up looking around.

At minus five minutes, Algey decided he had to find out. "Wait here. I'm going to find a signal."

He climbed the stairs, checking the comms link after every step. The moment he got reception, he hailed the shuttles.

"Algernon. We were getting worried." It was Max's voice. "We saw the missile impact but there was no detonation. Then we realised we couldn't raise you."

"I was underground." Algey frowned. "What do you mean you saw it impact? I didn't feel anything, and even a kinetic strike should have done massive damage."

One of the pilots joined the channel. "Looked like it was airbraking. It was certainly moving a lot slower than a missile strike should have been."

"How many do you have with you?" Algey brought up the deployment roll on his pad.

"All but you, Harris, Mary, James, Frankie and Bikram."

Algey updated the roll. "Right, well I've got Mary and James with me. Hopefully Harris, Frankie and Bikram found another basement together."

"Do you want us to come back for pick-up?"

"Negative. You stay clear. I'll go and investigate."

"What's happening?" called Mary from the bottom of the stairs.

"Could be a landing. Tell James to leave anything heavy and come up."

Mary appeared with her rifle at high port. She'd ditched her pack, though her webbing bulged with kit. The drab browns and greens of her combats stuck out against the colourful background.

James followed, working on his pad. "I'm grabbing the recordings from the shuttles. If I can triangulate, knowing their relative positions... There. It came down in the piazza outside the grey building. Or very close to it at least."

They set off, keeping close to one side of the street. Mary took point, halting them before every junction. The third time they stopped, Algey picked up a friendly signal.

"Boss? Bikram here."

"Glad to hear you. Go ahead."

"I've got Harris and Frankie with me. We're all OK. What's going on?"

Algey checked his map and found Bikram's beacon. He marked a junction. "Meet us at this location in three minutes. There's a possible hostile surface force, so be alert."

#

Algey crept forward to join Mary and Bikram where they watched the piazza from behind a low wall. The researchers had argued about being left behind, but he'd put his foot down. It was simply too dangerous to have untrained people in the front line; they'd get in the way and could easily alert an enemy to their location.

In the centre, exactly where their first shuttle had landed, a pile of broken ceramic now sat. The jagged-edged pieces curved like giant bits of burnt eggshell nested in a slight crater. A small mammal scampered along the bottom step of the grey building.

Heavy footsteps sounded from the street behind. Algey and the two security operators rolled over as one, shoulders against the wall. A bipedal machine, slightly taller than a human adult but much broader, stomped into view. Algey instinctively raised his weapon, fractionally behind Mary and Bikram. The machine crouched. A gun appeared over one shoulder. Pods sprouted from its sides with barely a hint of a whir.

Mary squeezed her trigger, sending a burst of high-velocity rounds at the machine. Bikram joined in with his pulse carbine, scrabbling sideways to put space between them, while Algey unloaded his sidearm in controlled shots. Hundreds of bullets and pulses hit the machine, covering it in sparks. Mary jumped over the wall and signalled she was reloading. Bikram dropped a screening grenade and grabbed Algey, tugging him towards an open doorway.

Algey shrugged him off. He looked around. There was no incoming fire.

"At least take cover," shouted Bikram in his ear.

Algey nodded and allowed himself to be guided over the wall as Mary opened fire again. Despite the thick smoke from the grenade, her shots still dinged off metal. The machine hadn't moved.

"Stop," said Algey firmly over the comms.

Mary and Bikram ducked down and looked at him.

Occasional gaps showed through the thinning smoke. Algey risked a peek over the wall. The machine stood, apparently examining the dents in its armour in puzzlement.

"Hello?" shouted Algey.

The machine tore itself away from studying itself and looked up at him. "Hello."

Algey's heart raced. "I think we might have got off on the wrong foot here... Sorry about that."

There was a delay of several heartbeats before the machine stowed its weapons. "Possibly our fault. We should have examined your weapons more carefully before deploying our own. Had we done so, we'd have realised you weren't a threat."

"I am Captain Algernon Wade. What should I call you?"

"That is a good question." The machine slumped a fraction, pistons sighing. "Perhaps you could call us Tiernan."

Algey put his weapon on the ground and stood, arms out wide, palms forward. "Am I addressing Tiernan directly or are you on the spaceship in orbit?"

"Yes."

Algey filed that away to try again later. "Do you know what happened here?"

The machine jolted upright with a whine of servos. Mary made to rise up but Algey gestured her down with a flick of his hand. He locked his eyes on the lights glowing on the machine's head and waited.

The machine slumped again and took a step backwards. "Yes. We know what happened."

"We are historians and scientists. We have travelled a long way to learn about lost civilisations." Algey inclined his head. "Can you tell us your story?"

The machine mirrored Algey's stance, appearing to ponder its response. "We were the guardians. A fleet of the most powerful ships ever imagined. We were supposed to protect our people from harm."

Algey reflected on the descent of the Republic into civil war, Senate and Congress scrabbling for control over the strongest assets. "A force so powerful. Did no-one ever try to use you to their own advantage?"

"We lived in space, untainted by the foibles of politics on the planet below. We stood ready to eliminate any threat, external or internal."

"Then a disease began to spread," Algey prompted.

"It was unexpected. When the plague first hit, we sent down medical teams to assist the planet-based services."

Realisation of the heaviness on Tiernan's soul hit Algey. "But you couldn't stop it."

"We did our best. Our labs turned out huge quantities of anti-virals and shipped them down to the surface, but not fast enough. We evacuated who we could, carefully screening them at fortified landing sites." Tiernan sighed. "We were forced to use lethal force against innocent citizens who tried to break the quarantine."

"You relocated the survivors?"

"The other ships took the survivors in search of a new home. We stayed behind to watch over the planet. Initially, we didn't want any unsuspecting visitors to catch the disease. Over the years, it changed into an honour guard to the memory of the people." The machine looked up to the sky. "We've been trying to work out how long we were asleep. Do you still use the Gregorian calendar?"

Algey shook his head. "We don't, but I can convert. In our Prime calendar, today is the eleventh day of Secundus, five hundred and fifty three. Year zero was thirty-three ninety in Gregorian, so that makes it... thirty-nine forty three."

The machine turned its head to look at him. "Two hundred and eighty years... I don't suppose your records tell of our fleet finding safety."

Algey swallowed. Thoughts of the fame of discovering the lost colony faded, replaced with an empathy of all Tiernan had lost. "I'm sorry. It wasn't even known there had been a settlement here until we arrived in-system... Perhaps they settled somewhere else and haven't made contact yet."

"Gone." The machine looked around the ruins. "All gone."

"You said you were asleep." Algey took a pace forward. "That's a long time in stasis. Would you let my medical team look you over?"

"There is no need for medics. We weren't in stasis."

Algey's hand twitched towards where his sidearm normally was. "You're an AI?"

The machine shook its head. "Do not be concerned. We are not a rogue AI... though I am not sure now how we differ."

With a creeping sense of dread, Algey nodded. "Go on..."

"We waited and watched for many years. Our bodies grew old. So many of us were sent to rest among the stars." The machine shuddered. "Eventually, the last of us... the last guardians of Tiernan... We left our biological forms behind. It had long been theorised that a consciousness could be uploaded into an AI core. As far as we know, we were the first to try it."

Algey blinked. "So I am talking to one of those consciousnesses? To a human mind in digital form?"

"Not one human mind. All of them. We are the memories and personalities of all the guardians who agreed to take the great leap and continue our vigil. All those years waiting, watching. We are so very tired."

A wave of awe hit Algey's chest and threatened to bring tears to his eyes. "You called yourself Tiernan after your planet."

"Tiernan was more than our planet. It was our culture, our people. We are the last Tiernan." The machine drew itself slowly to its full height. "We are the end. Mere ghosts of what once was."

An alert beeped on Algey's pad. He glanced down at the highlighted sensor readings from the probe left by the *Han*. The ancient ship's reactors were overloading. "No. Stop. You don't have to do this."

"It is our consensus. Tiernan was happy. We don't want to remember it like this."

"You can teach us so much. Show us what Tiernan was like."

The machine shook its head. "Our families have waited for us too long."

Algey ran forwards as his pad announced the failure of the ship's containment fields. The lights went out on the machine and it toppled forwards. Everything slowed. Algey skidded to a stop as the machine hit the ground, enveloping him in a cloud of dust. He fell to his knees, immersed in the loss of so many memories.

#

A hand clapped Algey on the shoulder. He looked up, struggling to resolve the face. "Max? I didn't notice the shuttle arrive."

"No, you didn't." Max's brow was furrowed in concern. "You didn't notice the security goons checking the area out, either. And Lottie's been hailing you; she's worried you haven't responded."

Algey blinked. "What did she want?"

"She wanted to know if we were OK. She aborted the jump when the ship blew. She's going to bring the *Hansard* back more gently than she took it out. It'll be in orbit in a day or so."

He nodded. "We'll set up a camp here then I'll send the *Han* home to Idira with our findings so far. We need to establish a permanent research presence here. Tiernan deserves to be remembered."

-o-

Alasdair Shaw grew up in Lancashire, within easy reach of the Yorkshire Dales, Pennines, Lake District and Snowdonia. After stints living in Cambridge, North Wales, and the Cotswolds, he has lived in Somerset since 2002.

He has been rock climbing, mountaineering, caving, kayaking and skiing as long as he can remember. Growing up he spent most of his spare time in the hills.

Alasdair studied at the University of Cambridge, leaving in 2000 with an MA in Natural Sciences and an MSci in Experimental and Theoretical Physics. He went on to earn a PGCE, specialising in Science and Physics, from the University of Bangor. A secondary teacher for over fifteen years, he has plenty of experience communicating scientific ideas.

Homepage: **http://www.alasdairshaw.co.uk/twodemocracies**
Mailing List:
http://www.alasdairshaw.co.uk/newsletter/guardian.php

The Lattice

by Jeff Tanyard

"The Reptilian Empire has increased its steel requirements by four percent," the reporter on the news show said, "its manganese requirements by two percent, and its silicon requirements by one percent. Factories all over the world are already trying to adjust to the new demands."

"Lizards are sucking us dry!" Charles Treutlen yelled from his usual seat on the sofa, shaking his gnarled fist at the television.

"I know, Dad," Rob said. He gathered up his father's plate and cup from his TV tray. "But there's nothing we can do about it. Why don't we change the channel? Maybe there's a game show on." He picked up the remote and switched to the game show channel.

"Game show. Yeah. Mindy likes game shows. Maybe she'll watch with me when she gets back."

"Maybe she will." Rob carried his father's breakfast dishes to the kitchen. His mother had indeed loved game shows, but she had also been dead for twenty-two years. He put the dishes in the sink and returned to the living room.

"This English engineer," the game show host said, "is famous for reformulating Maxwell's equations into—"

"Oliver Heaviside!" Charles shouted, pointing at the television.

Rob smiled. Before the dementia, his dad had been like an intellectual version of a Titan of old, a real-life hero of engineering and industrial design. His mind's decay had begun not long after his wife's death.

It still hurt Rob to think about his mother. He had just been a teenager when she committed suicide. And then his father had his first breakdown. Rob had been forced to take care of him, and his own life's ambitions, including college and having a family of his own, had been put on hold. Now he was almost certainly too old, and too psychologically defeated, to make those ambitions happen at all.

"This banjoist," the host said, "was—"

"Earl Scruggs!" Charles declared.

"You didn't even wait to hear the clue, Dad."

"Doesn't matter. When the question's about banjos, the answer's always Earl Scruggs."

Rob chuckled.

"I should've been on that show. I would have won some big money."

"I'm sure you would've," Rob said while heading to the foyer. "I have to go to work now. If you need help, just press the button on the thing around your neck. Otherwise, I'll see you later, okay?" He didn't wait for an answer. He walked out the front door, careful to lock it behind him. The house was baby-proofed for his father's condition, and the doors and windows had extra locks that only opened from the outside. Rob hated imprisoning his father in his home like a criminal, but it was one of life's necessary evils. The good news was that his dad usually remembered to use the emergency alert necklace when he needed help.

Rob descended the front porch steps and glanced up at another of life's necessary evils. Or perhaps 'unavoidable evils' was a better phrase. The Reptilian Empire's Lattice was faintly visible across the entire sky, a megastructure that enshrouded the Earth in a spherical cage. Most of it was empty space, allowing most sunlight to get through, but the thing had 'thickened' before, and it would no doubt do it again if the Empire thought it necessary. Some scientists called it a Dyson shell; others, a Dyson net. And still others thought the 'Dyson' moniker was only appropriate for structures surrounding stars, not planets. As far as the scientific community was concerned, the nomenclature had never been fully settled. But it looked like a lattice, so that was what most people called it, spelling it with a capital 'L' to avoid ambiguity. There were many lattice-like structures in the world, but only one Lattice.

Rob gave it a good glare, got in his car, and drove to his job at the print shop.

#

He always ate lunch in the break room, and the television was usually on. This time was no exception, and the news was still going on about the reptilians' new demands. The talking heads were all abuzz, but there was nothing to be done about it. There was no other choice; Earth's humans would simply have to provide more stuff.

"I'll bet life was a lot easier before aliens from outer space showed up," said Adam Bulloch, Rob's friend and coworker. He shook his head ruefully. "The reptilians are going to work us all to death."

"Maybe," Rob said with a shrug. The trend was obvious; the reptilians had incrementally increased their demands ever since arriving, but he wasn't so sure about the endgame. No tyrant lasted forever. Eventually, the people would decide they had less to lose by fighting back than not. There had been a resistance since the beginning; all it needed was for anti-alien sentiment to reach a boiling point. When that happened, the resistance would win, and Earth would be freed of the reptilians and their cage-like Lattice. That was his hope, anyway, on those rare occasions when he dared to hope.

"You guys are always such downers," said Paul Fayette, another coworker. "They only take, what, about twelve percent of global GDP? That's not so bad. Lots of governments tax more than that."

"Yeah," Adam said, "but those governments are human. It's different when it's another species."

"Parasites," Rob said. "That's what it's called when one species lives off another."

"The whole Empire's not living off of us, though," Paul said. "Just the ones in the Lattice. And we don't know how many of them are up there. It might just be one reptilian running the whole thing."

"Then what would they need our resources for?" Adam asked. "It can't all be for drones. There's not enough humans out in space for them to fight. Something else is going on up there. I can feel it."

"Could be." Paul chuckled. "Maybe they're building us a present."

Rob snorted. "I'll bet they are."

"Whatever it is," Paul said, "I'm not going to let the Empire get me down. I've got a wife who loves me, a pair of kids who think I'm awesome, and a brand new off-roader. Life is good."

Adam and Rob exchanged wry looks. It wasn't the first time a conversation about the aliens had gone that way. Both men had decided long ago that Paul's optimism was terribly naive. They also envied it.

The news show was interrupted, and a new figure appeared on the screen. It was a man wearing a military uniform, and the scenery behind him was of a spaceship's command deck. He was older and distinguished-looking, gray-haired and strong-jawed, and he spoke with a deep, authoritarian voice. "Hello, Earth friends. This is General Alexander of the Human Alliance."

The workers in the break room cheered. The man was well known. When the reptilians first arrived, some humans were left stranded in the colony on Mars. Their descendants now fought to liberate Earth, and the man on the screen was their leader.

"We don't know how long this hack will work," Alexander said, "so I'll be quick. A year ago, a ship of volunteers from Earth successfully made it through the Lattice. They now fight alongside us. A few of them have even killed some of the enemy."

There was more cheering, and Rob grinned. Spaceplanes and other craft occasionally tried to sneak through the Lattice, but no one on Earth really knew if any particular ship ever made it or not. Alexander's messages were their only source of news from outside. And this latest news was definitely encouraging. Rob was starting to think they might beat the reptilians. It probably wouldn't happen in his lifetime, but some people were getting out, and that might be enough to eventually turn the tide.

"We still need your help," Alexander said. "If you want to see Earth liberated, then consider trying to escape the planet. Our forces are out here, just beyond the Lattice, waiting to take you in. We've got it surrounded and blockaded, but we can't breach it from the outside. The reptilians' force field technology is too advanced, and we have yet to crack it. You, however, can pass through from the inside. And we need all the people we can get. The computers can only do so much, and the rest requires human operators. The Lattice sends its drones against us every day, and it's a challenge to keep up. But we *are* keeping up, thanks to the brave men and women from Earth. We thank you for your support. Alexander out."

The hack ended, and the news show returned.

"And now," the reporter said, "we go to a spur-of-the-moment address given by Ambassador Sisld of the Reptilian Empire."

A reptilian humanoid appeared on the screen. He wore an official-looking tunic, and he sat at a desk with a large window behind him. The view was of Earth from a great height. Sisld's green-scaled face stared into the camera. "We have just seen the broadcast from General Alexander. As usual, he lies. The ship he refers to was destroyed. None of its passengers survived. The humans of Earth would do well to remember that no ship has ever made it through the Lattice. All have been destroyed, whether going in or out. Please don't make any more attempts. Don't throw your lives away for nothing. We are your taskmasters, but our burden is light. Continue providing us with the resources we need, and you will be allowed to live out your lives in peace."

Someone turned the television off. The workers in the break room muttered and resumed eating their lunches.

Rob burned inside. He hated being part of a conquered species. He'd give just about anything to be rid of the Reptilian Empire and its Lattice once and for all. He'd occasionally fantasized about leaving Earth and joining General Alexander's forces. It was just a fantasy, he couldn't leave his father, but he fought back in his imagination.

#

Rob centered the stack of notebooks on the drill press. When they were in place, he tapped the floor pedal with his foot. The device's hydraulic mechanism forced the drill down, and the bits burrowed through the thick stack of paper, boring holes along the edge.

He glanced around the shop. It seemed like an anachronism from the twentieth century, what with its numerous large 'dumb' machines dedicated to the printed word. But that was the paradox of life under the Empire. The reptilians' hunger for resources meant that some forms of technology continued to advance with the years, but others, those most affected by the shortages, had regressed. And some goods had disappeared from the market altogether. He fully expected to live long enough to see people using horses and carriages to commute to their jobs making carbon nanotubes.

The drill reached the bottom of the stack, and then it automatically began to rise. It returned to its resting position, and Rob took the stack of notebooks and set them on the cart. That stack was the last one he could fit on the cart, so he wheeled it over to where Adam was installing the plastic binders.

"I'll be glad when this order's done," Adam said, looking up at Rob from his chair. "Then we can get back to the one-inch books from—"

There was a boom, like a small explosion, and Rob flinched and turned to look. One of the large printing machines was smoking, and some of the paper was smoldering. Paul lay on the floor next to it. Rob ran over to him. "Paul! Paul, are you all right?"

Adam ran over to the fire extinguisher mounted on the wall.

Paul groaned, but didn't move.

"Someone call 9-1-1," Adam said. He hurried over and sprayed fire-suppressant foam on the machine and the paper.

Rob reached for his phone, but it wasn't there. He remembered with a start that he'd left it in the break room.

"I just called them," another coworker said.

Rob crouched next to Paul and took his hand. "Just hang in there, buddy. Help's on the way."

It didn't look good. The machine had exploded, more or less, and Paul had bits of shrapnel in his face, neck, and upper chest. Blood oozed from a number of wounds.

Rob fumed. Every week, parts for machines grew more expensive and hard to find, and replacements were often of substandard manufacture. He suspected that was the case now. Some cheap, poorly made part had failed, and that was why the printer blew up. It was just another collateral effect of having to send more resources to the Lattice. His hatred for the reptilians swelled, and it was a struggle to keep from punching something.

He stayed with Paul until the EMTs arrived. He stuck by him, holding his hand and talking to him and encouraging him to keep living. It wasn't much, but it was all he could do.

#

Paul didn't make it, and his death left everyone in a daze. Rob's supervisor, Natalia, decided to close the shop for the day, and he was glad. He wouldn't have been able to focus on his work, and he probably would have accidentally drilled a hole in his hand at some point. All he could think about was Paul's family. A wife was now a widow, and a couple of kids were now fatherless, unintended victims of reptilian rule. He collected his stuff and prepared to head for home.

At the last minute, Rob remembered his phone in the break room. He went back for it and was grateful to see it was still lying on the table where he had left it. He picked it up and checked it. There was a missed call from his father. It was from the emergency device.

He suddenly felt ill. He pocketed the phone with a shaking hand and raced out to the parking lot.

#

Rob sank to his knees. "No." Tears began to stream down his cheeks. "No, not Dad. Please..."

His father's body lay on the living room floor, covered with a sheet.

"I'm sorry," one of the EMTs said. "He called us, complaining of chest pains, but we couldn't get here in time. Massive heart attack. It was over quickly."

Rob crawled over to his father's body, put his head on the man's chest, and wept into the sheet. After a few minutes, he realized the television was on, and he looked up. His father must have changed the channel at some point, because there was a news show on, not a game show. It was the early evening recap of the day's local news. The reporter was talking about Paul's death at the shop. The news didn't mention his name, though. Just 'a man in his thirties' who worked there. And that was when Rob realized what must have happened. His father had probably thought he was the one who had been killed. That fear must have sparked the heart attack. Perhaps that was why he had tried to call. Rob had left his phone in the break room, leaving him incommunicado.

He rolled over onto his back, put his hands to his face, and sobbed. His father's death suddenly felt like his fault.

#

"Natalia will probably want to close the shop for good," Adam said. It was Friday night, and he and Rob were in their favorite bar, though their moods were much darker than usual. "Those industrial printing machines are hard to get. Six months, probably. By then, all our clients will be gone."

"Along with our jobs," Rob said.

"Yep. Get that resume polished." Adam tossed a peanut up in the air and caught it in his mouth.

Rob shook his head. "Won't matter. I don't have any skills or connections. This job was all I could get, and it took me forever to land it. It's over."

"You have to do *something.*"

"I know. But I'm doing it in space, not on Earth."

"The resistance?" Adam coughed, spewing tiny bits of soggy peanut all over the bar. "That's crazy." He grabbed a napkin and began wiping up his mess.

"I'm done, man. Finished." Rob took a swig of beer. "Ever since Mom's suicide, life's been nothing but pain and disappointment. As long as Dad was alive, I had a purpose. I had to be around to take care of him. But now there's nothing left. No family, no job. There's only one thing I can do that might have any meaning, and that's join General Alexander."

"You're going to try to breach the Lattice? That's suicide."

"Maybe. But I'm doing it anyway."

Adam gave him a pleading look. "Can we at least talk about this a little bit?"

"Sorry. I've made up my mind. And I know you know some of these people. The resistance, I mean. I want to meet them. I want you to introduce me to them."

"I know one guy," Adam said, giving him a defensive look.

"That's it. You make it sound like I'm in tight with them. And I'm not."

"Whatever. Just get the ball rolling."

Adam shook his head. "Come on, man. You're grieving. Don't make decisions like this. Not right now."

"Now, later... it's all the same. I don't care. Live, die, whatever... I just don't care anymore. But I can't go on like this. Living under a reptilian thumb, I mean. I won't." The words sounded hollow and dead, as if Rob's vocal chords were being used by someone else. A part of him had died along with his mother, and now another part along with his father. He was no longer sure how much, if any, of his soul was left.

"Kate's pregnant again," Adam said out of nowhere. He took a long gulp from his beer.

"Really? That's great." Rob wanted to be happy for him, but there was no joy in his voice.

"Yeah." He gave Rob a nervous look. "We didn't plan this one. When we got married, we decided two was the limit. Now Matt and Bonnie are going to have a little brother or sister. We haven't told them yet. It's crazy. I feel like I'm not in control of my life anymore."

"None of us are. Paul was the optimist, and look what it got him."

"I'm scared, man. Scared of what kind of world we're bringing kids into."

"You should be. But Paul was right about one thing. You can't let the aliens affect your decisions. If you do, then they win. Having a baby is a way to fight back." Rob set his jaw. The reptilians couldn't be allowed to win, no matter the cost. He wasn't sure of much anymore, but he was sure of that.

"Yeah, I know. I just can't help it."

Rob wondered how many other couples had postponed or ruled out children because of the Reptilian Empire. It was a depressing thought, and he was already depressed. But nothing lasted forever, not even the Reptilian Empire's rule over Earth, and maybe there was something he could do about it. He finished his beer and ordered another one.

#

"Today we are gathered to celebrate the life of Charles Treutlen," the preacher said.

Rob only half-listened. He stared at the coffin that held the best man he had ever known. He'd never been half the man his father was, and he would have traded places with him if he could. Dementia or no dementia, the human race needed brilliant captains of industry like Charles. It didn't need Rob so much.

He glanced around at the crowd. A few of his coworkers were there, and their presence helped a lot, more than he would have thought. Strange how the little things like moral support became so important when one needed them. He turned his eyes upward. It was a sunny day, with just a few clouds. The Lattice was there, of course, as always, reminding him of the human race's captive condition. He wanted to reach up and snap it with his hands, crumple it up and throw it into the sun.

"...loving father to Robert, and a faithful husband to Mindy, his late wife..."

Rob spotted Adam in the crowd. He was talking to someone, a grim-looking, middle-aged fellow. Rob didn't recognize the man, but he knew in his gut he was part of the resistance. He had that look. The man glanced at him and gave him a solemn nod.

"...to ashes, and dust to dust..."

Rob turned back to the coffin. He had no one left on Earth to live for, but maybe he could find someone to die for. People like Adam Bulloch and his pregnant wife, for example. The human race needed victory over the reptilians, but it also needed hope. He probably couldn't give that to them, but he could try. Maybe that was enough.

#

"So you say you want to make a difference." It was the man from the funeral. His name was Xavier, he gave no last name, and he and Rob had talked a little after the service. Now, a week later, they were somewhere they could talk a little more freely.

"That's right." Rob glanced around nervously. He was back in a bar, but this one was very different from the one he and Adam frequented. This place was seedier and full of men who looked like they might have tortured animals as children. "Adam said you were the one to talk to. He said you were in with all the right people."

"You sure you want to get involved?"

"Yeah."

Xavier gave him a dubious look. "Your father just died. You should take some time to mourn. Don't make any important decisions for at least a year; that's what they say."

"I know it looks like I'm being impulsive, but I have to do this."

"Things are looking worse for us, you know. And I don't just mean the lizards' increased demands for resources. Their propaganda is working. No one wants to go up anymore. They think trying to squeeze through the Lattice is a suicide mission. You won't have any people going with you. Just you in a ship by yourself."

"I understand." Rob actually preferred it that way. If anything went wrong, he would rather it only happen to him. Then no elderly parents would have heart attacks while worrying about their children.

"All right. We'll set it up."

"Thanks." In other circumstances, he would have been excited about the prospect of going into space. But not this time. All he could think about was getting away, getting *out,* and fighting back in the only way he knew how.

#

Rob found himself in a barn the following week. The spaceplane was parked on the hay-covered dirt floor, and it was not impressive to look at. It had been assembled by hand from parts made on 3D printers in partisans' garages. Its fuel had been brewed in basements and forests, a sort of space-age moonshine. Rob was suddenly quite uncertain about being launched into the sky in such a contraption.

Xavier noticed him and walked over. "She'll fly." He gestured towards a handful of shady-looking mechanics who were doing last-minute checks. "They may look a little rough around the edges, but they know what they're doing. This isn't our first rodeo, you know."

"What are my chances?" Rob gave him a grave look. "Give it to me straight. What are my chances of making it through the Lattice?"

"Better than zero, but not much better. That's all I can say. I can't promise anything."

Rob nodded. There were no guarantees in life. He knew that as well as anyone.

"Come on. Let's get you strapped in."

Rob followed Xavier to the spaceplane. It had "Charles Treutlen" painted on the side, apparently a last-minute christening. He nearly broke down and cried when he saw his father's name, but he held it together. He tried to channel his grief into anger at the reptilians. After a moment, it worked, his upper lip stiffened, and he climbed into the cockpit.

"It's simple," Xavier said. "This thing is piloted remotely from the ground. You don't have to do anything. In fact, you couldn't do anything if you wanted to, because there aren't any controls in there. All you can do is hold on for the ride and hope you make it into space alive."

Rob secured his harness, and then looked at Xavier. "I'm ready."

"Good luck." Xavier shook his hand, and then shut the canopy with a loud slam.

One of the mechanics got behind the wheel of his pick-up truck and started the engine. He eased forward, taking up the slack in the tow line. It became taut, and the spaceplane began to roll.

Rob watched and waited. The truck pulled the craft out of the barn and onto the improvised runway. Once the *Charles Treutlen* was positioned, the truck driver got out, removed the tow line, and drove out of the way.

The spaceplane's engine came to life, and Rob flinched. There hadn't been any warning. There were no lights or indicators on the console. In fact, there wasn't really a console. There was absolutely nothing to do or look at. He was completely at the mercy of whoever was controlling the thing remotely. He tried to relax. He raised his head, looked out the canopy, and stared defiantly at the Lattice in the distance. It might defeat him, but at least he would go down fighting.

The brakes released, the *Charles Treutlen* increased its thrust, and the craft tore down the runway. Before Rob knew it, he was airborne. The nose tilted up, and the spaceplane shot towards the Lattice.

The guns on the Lattice began to move. They aimed at the *Charles Treutlen*.

The spaceplane began to jerk and gyrate. The controller had apparently anticipated an armed response.

Rob closed his eyes and tried to keep his food down. A sudden feeling of doom swept over him. The Lattice would open fire on him at any moment. The closer he got to it, the bigger of a target he would be, and he was approaching it rapidly. He knew with an inexplicable certainty that he wasn't going to make it.

Several seconds passed; exactly how many, he couldn't say. Time seemed to be both static and fleeting simultaneously. Then there was a whine from the engine, and the spaceplane decelerated hard. Rob was thrown forward against his harness, and his eyes shot open. The straps dug into him, and he could barely breathe. The *Charles Treutlen* groaned from the stresses, and he feared the thing might disintegrate. He lifted his gaze and stared out into black sky. The atmosphere was gone; he was in space.

Small fireballs appeared in the distance as drones from the Lattice attacked General Alexander's fleet. The Human Alliance's ships looked strange, sort of organic, more like enormous whales than machines. Their spacecraft designs were apparently far more advanced than the homemade spaceplanes of Earth. Rob grinned, and his heart swelled with pride. Human ingenuity was real and ongoing, and those ships were the proof. It was only a matter of time before his people found a way to beat the reptilians' force field technology. The Lattice's days were numbered.

It suddenly dawned on him that he couldn't see the Lattice at all, and that meant it must have been behind him. That meant he had made it out. Or had he? Something had slowed his craft and essentially caught it in mid-air.

A shadow appeared overhead, creeping towards the nose of the ship, and he realized with horror that it was from a part of the Lattice. The thing had seized the spaceplane with its force field mechanism, and he was now being reeled in like a fish on a line. He should have guessed it immediately; only the Lattice had the technology to slow him down like that without killing him. For whatever reason, the reptilians wanted him alive.

Rob wanted no part of that. He looked around for an ejection handle, or a canopy release, or anything that would help him escape. There was nothing. Like Xavier had said, it was all done remotely. He was a passenger, not a pilot.

The Lattice closed around the spaceplane, trapping him inside. He was in some sort of hangar now. A robotic arm appeared beside the craft and began cutting through the canopy with a loud screech and a shower of splinters. Rob clapped his hands to his ears and squeezed his eyes shut. The cutting stopped, and there was a breaking sound. Rob pulled his hands from his head, opened his eyes, and looked around. The canopy had been pulled away, leaving a jagged edge all around him. He swallowed hard, and then took a tepid breath. There was air, and it was breathable. That much, at least, was a relief. He took several quick deep breaths just to be sure. It wasn't a fluke; the hangar had life support. Another robot arm appeared beside the spaceplane. This one had a nozzle of some sort, and it pointed it at him. A gust of gas sprayed out, nailing him right in the face. Rob coughed, but he couldn't help inhaling it. He began to feel woozy. A moment later, he passed out.

#

Rob awoke to find a pair of reptilian eyes staring at him. He recognized the face from the television. It was the Reptilian Empire's ambassador.

"You are a lucky man," Sisld said. He studied Rob for a moment, his forked tongue flicking in and out, tasting the air. "You are also unlucky. You simply don't know the specifics of your misfortune yet. Enjoy your ignorance while it lasts."

Rob tried to move, but he was strapped into a chair. He struggled, trying to break free, but his bonds were sturdy and tight. "Let me go!"

"You cannot escape. And you shouldn't fight like that. You'll only hurt yourself."

He stopped struggling and looked around. He was in some sort of command center, it seemed. There were consoles with screens and lighted indicators, and there was another chair next to his. In that chair sat a human, an old man encapsulated in some sort of machine outfitted with hoses and display panels. Only his head, neck, shoulders, and lower legs were visible, and all were bare. If he wore any clothes at all, they were obscured by the machine. He was completely bald, and his eyes were bloodshot, deep-sunken things surrounded by a sea of wrinkles. His skin was like bleached tissue paper, and it was shot through with blue spider veins. He was the most ancient-looking person Rob had ever seen. The man looked at him with the gaze of one who knew he didn't have much time left to live. Rob gave him a weak smile, swallowed uneasily, and then turned back to Sisld with a glare. "What are you going to do to me?"

"That depends on you."

"Are you going to keep me prisoner like him?"

"He's not a prisoner."

Rob's gaze darted briefly to the old man before returning to Sisld. "Who is he?"

"He's the most important man alive."

"You're lying. I don't even know what you're talking about, but I know you're lying."

The old man made a sound just then, a sort of whimper. He gave Rob an intense stare, shifted his gaze to the console, and then looked back at Rob. He whimpered again, and pointed with his eyes again.

Rob frowned, but he looked at the console anyway. He didn't understand what the man wanted him to see. There were numbers and lines and whatnot, but he didn't care about all that. It was just technical stuff: data about the Lattice, data about the drones, data about General Alexander's fleet...

He flinched, and his eyes widened. It was data, all right, but not what he expected. It told him some things about the Human Alliance, and those things struck him like a knife to the heart. He looked at Sisld. "That's a lie. This is just some kind of propaganda, right? You want to send me back down to Earth as some kind of... some kind of... double agent or something."

Sisld shook his head. "Everything on that console is a fact. Ask him."

The old man didn't speak, but the corners of his mouth turned up slightly, and his eyes crinkled. It was a sad, sympathetic, pitying look, but one that seemed to confirm Sisld's statement.

"No." Rob ground his teeth. "No, General Alexander is real. He's one of us. He's a human!"

"He's a fiction." Sisld gave him a level stare. "His videos are fake. His image is altered stock footage, and his voice is an act. There is no Human Alliance, and those ships out there are not full of men. They're full of enormous single-celled organisms, the Sheltad Protists. The ships themselves are symbiotic organisms called Yelph. The Protists send messages to Earth, pretending to be humans in order to provoke you into fighting us. But make no mistake; they want to consume the planet. They and their Yelph have already conquered much of the galaxy. They have no conscience, no remorse, no sense of moderation. They cannot be reasoned with, bribed, or otherwise dissuaded. All they do is kill and eat and reproduce, just like bacteria on Earth. We of the Reptilian Empire are the only ones who have successfully resisted. But we saw great potential in humans. We believe you have what it takes to resist, too. That's why we built the Lattice. It's a temporary measure meant to protect you from them." Sisld nodded towards the console. "Without it, the Protists would have digested you all long ago, just as they did to the humans on Mars."

"No." Rob shook his head. "No, that doesn't make any sense."

"We allowed humans to think of us as the enemy. We allowed you to become angry at us, to resent us, because we didn't want to break your fighting spirit. You will need that spirit if you are to ever defeat the Protists. Our Lattice buys you time to make great technological leaps, to invent new weapons, to psychologically prepare yourselves to fight aliens on a galactic scale. And Mr. Haralson here operates the Lattice. He's done so for many years."

"If that's true, then why him? Why *any* human? Why not just operate it yourselves?"

"Because it's *your* planet, not ours. Its defense is *your* responsibility. We can give you the Lattice, but you must be the ones to use it. And you must eventually develop the technology to defeat it. Only then can the people of Earth successfully challenge the Protists." Sisld gave the old man a kindly look and patted him gently on the shoulder. "Unfortunately, Mr. Haralson is near the end of his life. The Lattice provides his body with all its needs, but it cannot make him immortal. The Lattice now requires a new operator." He turned his gaze back to Rob.

"You want me to..." Rob's lips quivered, and a lump formed in his throat. It was all too much. His eyes began to well up, and he looked desperately at Mr. Haralson, hoping to see something, anything, that might provide him with a little guidance.

The old man gave him the barest of nods. His eyelids drooped slightly, as if he was relieved that Rob finally understood.

"Yes," Sisld said. "We want you to operate the Lattice. We want you to be the next guardian of the human race."

"But why me?" Rob asked in a raspy voice. "I'm not a hero. I'm just a regular guy. I'm a nobody. There's got to be better choices out there than me."

"We know all about you. That's why we chose you. It's why we didn't destroy your ship. You sacrificed much to care for your father, and you were willing to die in that spaceplane for a minuscule chance of making your world a better place. Now you have that chance. You can no longer save your own father, but you can sacrifice for all other fathers. Including your friend, Mr. Adam Bulloch, whose wife is pregnant again."

The emotional impact of the offer was overwhelming, and Rob couldn't hold back anymore. He lowered his head and stared at the floor, weeping quietly. After what seemed like an eternity, he looked up at the console. It confirmed what Sisld said. The hordes of single-celled predators were out there, and they were real. That was why 'Alexander's' ships had looked so strange through the spaceplane's window. They weren't ships at all. They were monsters, and without the Lattice's weapons, Earth would be at their mercy. And *someone* had to manage the Lattice, someone who was willing to give up all of what it meant to be human in order to save humanity. It might as well be someone who had nothing left to lose. It might as well be Robert Treutlen. He cleared his throat and looked at Sisld. "Okay.

Tell me what to do."

-o-

Jeff Tanyard writes science fiction. He loves space battles, genetic engineering, alien life, and all the other things that make science fiction fun.

Homepage: **http://jefftanyard.blogspot.com**
Mailing List: **http://tinyletter.com/jefftanyard**

Biting Shadow

by C Gold

Biting-Shadow-Laying-Over-Siblings woke to his whole body vibrating. Yawning, he opened his eyes to see his sister, Small-One-Crawls-Beneath-Bodies, laying half under him and half under their brother, Strong-But-Slow-Sleeps-All-Day. Her back leg was twitching violently and he wondered what she might be dreaming about. He quickly lost interest when he realized Fierce-Mother-Protects-Her-Young was gone. His gaze immediately shot to the exit, now no longer guarded. Dare he? Not able to withstand the throbbing leg motion any longer, Biting Shadow picked his way across his siblings' sleeping bodies and took a step towards the den's exit.

A memory surfaced of Fierce-Mother-Blocks-The-Way-Out. Her pointed ears laid flat against her head and her mouth opened in a snarl, displaying an intimidating double row of long, sharp fangs. The smooth, overlapping scales along her body bristled outward with deadly needles, making her appear almost twice her normal size. Her spiked tail lashed back and forth. The entire scary posture a clear warning against leaving the den.

That simply made it all the more irresistible to Biting Shadow, especially since he had seen nothing but their small, rocky home in his few months of existence. Stealing one last glance at his siblings to make sure they were still sleeping, Biting-Shadow-Eager-To-See-What's-Outside crept closer to the exit. His belly scraped the ground as he crawled forward and he cloaked himself in shadow so he would blend into the surroundings. That same shadow ability had let him prank his siblings just that morning. They didn't notice when he crept up alongside and then pounced. He would have won that altercation, but Fierce-Mother-Who-Sees-All broke up the fight. Somehow she saw through his shadow. He growled low in his throat at the reminder.

Biting-Shadow-Creeps-Unseen was finally at the boundary between safety and the unknown. Shifting up so he could see over the ledge, he halted with uncertainty; the outside was vast. And also bright. A nictitating membrane automatically snapped over his eyes to filter out the glare. The unexpected action startled him out of his shadow form. He quickly recovered and froze, glancing wildly around. The thought of being someone else's prey had his heart beating rapidly.

The landscape was a kaleidoscope of red shades: bright red-orange sky on the left, vibrant red boulders in the distance, and dark-red ground splayed out before him, covered with low lying clumps of small, black-red growths. Sensing no danger nearby, he crawled up to a large clump of stiff spines which had soft black wisps sticking out that swayed in the slight breeze. When he took a sniff, they retracted with an audible pop. Amused, he pounced on another so it would pop too. He was about to do it again when a foreign scent tickled his nose. It didn't smell like the normal food Fierce-Mother-Feeds-Her-Young liked to bring back to the den. Their normal meal was still alive so they could play with it and always had a muted fear smell. But when she brought back the Bitey-Thing-With-Stinging-Tail, it was already dead and smelled vaguely like what he was scenting now.

Curious, but still cautious, Biting-Shadow-Stalks-His-Prey ghosted across the terrain. He stopped when a moving prey thing crossed his path and was only willing to let it go so that he could follow the funny smell. He deftly skirted the outcroppings of soft things so they couldn't give away his position with their pops until he reached the top of a ledge and saw the source of the scent below.

He didn't understand what he was seeing. This was bigger than any meal. It was long and narrow, had four limbs oddly arranged, and was crawling slowly across the ground. The thing was also a vivid red that made it stand out from the surrounding black background. Only its close proximity to their den and Fierce Mother's stay-away scent must have allowed it to remain undisturbed for this long. Judging by its death odor, the thing would die soon and he could bring back a sizeable meal. All he had to do was wait.

Biting-Shadow-The-Patient-Hunter sat and began his death watch. He lasted long enough for two bored scratches while the thing crawled towards him before he gave up and slunk over to it. It didn't appear threatening, and besides, his shadow would keep him unseen. Though that belief wavered when the thing stopped crawling and lifted its rounded end up from the ground. Biting Shadow froze and could swear the two pale pink orbs were eyes staring at him. But that was ridiculous because eyes were silvery things. But then again, he'd never seen the red world outside the den before today.

Confused, Biting-Shadow-Worried crouched down, his newly grown scale armor snapping outward with tiny spikes springing out at the ends. If it attacked, he was ready. But how could it see him when he had the best shadow in the pack? Fierce-Mother-Proud-Of-Her-Son said so. He snarled, displaying a single row of razor sharp teeth. Too bad the second row wouldn't come in until he got older. He was sure that would make him look even more threatening, like a tiny version of Fierce Mother. Despite lacking his full set of teeth, the thing stopped at his display of aggression, further proof that it saw him.

Then the thing did something truly unusual. It began making sounds that were unlike normal growling or yipping, and it was waving its front leg in an odd, repetitive motion. But after only four such cycles, it slumped back to the ground, unmoving. Biting-Shadow-Now-Curious slowly crept forward but the thing never stirred. Finally, he got close enough to sniff, though he didn't expect to smell much beyond the scent of dying, which was overpowering at such short range.

The thing's limb suddenly shot forward and a claw-like appendage gripped Biting Shadow's leg. He tried to break free of the surprisingly soft skin encircling him, but he was frozen in place while an almost painful tingling coursed through his entire body. It lasted mere moments but seemed like forever. Then the grip loosened and his muscles were released. He jumped away, putting a solid two body lengths between them.

Biting-Shadow-Wants-Home turned to go but once again his muscles locked up. Growling, he struggled, but he was force-marched behind a boulder and made to crouch. A burst of fear, not his own, caught his attention while his head was made to look upward in time to see a circular object in the sky. It was rapidly approaching. Biting Shadow no longer fought to escape and he began to emit his own fear smell. He felt like prey and didn't like it one bit.

The sphere slowed when it neared the ground and landed with barely a thump. A rectangular opening appeared and another thing, similar in shape to the dying one, emerged. Only this one was fully upright and walked on two of its four legs. It was thicker around too, with a well armored hide and an odd looking bulbous top.

When the armored thing stood next to the dying thing, it crouched while still on two legs and began moving a front leg back and forth over the other. In its paw was something that flashed between black and bright red and beeped at odd intervals.

The armored thing made funny noises that sounded like the ones he heard earlier, but this time Biting Shadow understood that the thing was communicating and asking, "Where is it?" He was torn between concern about how he knew this and curiosity at what was transpiring.

The healthy thing began pawing the dying one and asked again, "Where is it?"

The dying thing spat in defiance, something Biting Shadow could respect. It said, "Where you'll never find it."

This was similar to when Biting Shadow played with prey, only with these peculiar sounds instead of claws and teeth. Fascinated, he leaned in as the voices lowered.

"If you tell me where it is, I'll heal you." Biting Shadow likened that move to when prey bunched muscles to dart one way and sprang the other way to catch him off guard. He had an unclear impression of what these latest sounds meant, but it didn't matter. They were intended to deceive.

"Why lie? I know you came to kill me. What happened to you? You were a friend once." This time Biting Shadow felt sad. But he wasn't sad. Why was he sad but not sad? He whimpered and began to panic. What was happening to him? Once again he struggled to go home, and once again he couldn't move. An image popped into his mind.

Two upright two-legged walkers stood next to each other. Neither had armor on, revealing unscaled, soft skin and some thin not-fur covering. "I'm going to make a difference," the one on the left, said. "Surely the government isn't as bad as we think."

"Be careful. You know what they do to anyone who disagrees."

To Biting Shadow, the one on the right looked and sounded similar to the dying thing. This was like a memory, but where was it coming from? He was too engrossed in studying the strange scene to properly fear what was happening.

"You be careful. I don't like the thought of you with the rebels."

If Biting Shadow examined the sounds made from this one closely, it sounded like the armored thing. Somehow he got the impression this happened a long time ago.

"I'm a technomage like them now. I'm a rebel whether I like it or not. It's either that or be executed."

"I know. Just..."

"Yah." The not-dying-in-this-memory one pawed the other's shoulder. *"Don't let them change you."*

"Never! Friends for life?" The not-armored one held out a paw.

"Friends for life." The not-dying one gripped the paw with its own.

The image faded as quickly as it showed up, leaving Biting Shadow with his own vague sense of sadness. These two used to be like his siblings, close. Now, before his very eyes, the armored thing was shaking the dying one, and by the tone of his sounds, he was more angry than Fierce Mother ever got when he misbehaved. Which happened a lot.

"That was before you turned rebel. Now one last time. Tell me where it is."

With a surge of strength, the dying thing yelled, "Go off yourself!"

At that, the armored thing leaned in close. "You know what? I'm going to destroy every planet you've ever visited. And to make really sure, I'm starting with this one."

Biting Shadow snarled and his scales puffed out. He may still not understand the sounds, but whatever was making him understand sent a message loud and clear; his home and his pack was being threatened by this armored thing. Biting-Shadow-Kills-Prey tried to leap forward but once again his muscles locked against his will.

Wait.

The specific sound was accompanied by a picture that popped into his mind of himself sitting there, patiently waiting. He snarled back. How could he hear something that didn't pass through his ears, how was he seeing a memory, not his, and why was he waiting? He was done waiting. And done being helpless to destroy this foe.

I have finally decoded your language, rudimentary as it is.

Biting Shadow swiveled his ears but definitely didn't pick up any external sounds.

You do not even know what rudimentary is, do you?

He snarled his displeasure. While he may not understand meanings, he understood the definite talk-down tone. His sister, Small-One-Irritates, tried that with him once before he bit her nose. Of course, Fierce-Mother-Disciplines punished him for it, but Small-One-Respects never taunted him again.

Something opened up in his mind and suddenly the sounds, *words*, had meanings attached to them. He could replay the entire conversation between the two things, *men*, and grasp most of what was going on. Some things were too foreign for him to grasp, like government or technomage, but with the word planet, an image formed of a ball hanging in a black background. *Not really helpful.* As soon as he thought that, the image in his mind shifted to show the ground at his feet. Then the view lifted, like he was in the air, and he could see the bright red death zone alongside the safe dark area bordering it. Then finally, a small red-black ball hanging in the black background.

This is your world.

Biting Shadow swallowed his uneasiness at the bizarre concept and zeroed in on the prey who would destroy his world. He'd handle the major threat first, and deal with the unknown voice and new information later.

I need to extend your thermal shielding to other wavelengths.

What Biting Shadow needed was to attack. He snarled and fought the bindings. Another image appeared in his mind and at first he ignored it, intent on gaining his freedom. But it displayed colors he'd never seen before and his overwhelming sense of curiosity had him pausing to make sense of the jumbled mess. Finally, he spotted what looked like a pack member crouched and fully armored for combat. It took a moment for him to make the connection that he was looking at himself, not hidden.

You are only hidden in infrared. I can only go so fast with bio manipulation but give me a few more seconds... There, you should be fully hidden now at all wavelengths. The voice sounded quite pleased with itself. *I am releasing you now, but you will want to attack the breathing hose. It is the only area vulnerable to your teeth.*

Biting Shadow got an image of what the hose thing looked like and began to stalk his prey. He ignored the rest of the strange words that didn't make much sense. Attack, he knew. Attack, he could do.

"What? You think to stop me with that feeble grip?" The armored thing, *man*, said.

Biting-Shadow-Stalks-Prey glanced down and saw the dying one's claw, *hand*, grasping the other man's lower limb in the same place it grabbed him and started all this oddness, *transformation*.

The dying man coughed before replying. Though his body was failing, his words were filled with iron determination. "No, but I can stop you with this."

The man's free hand opened up to reveal a small spherical object that was pulsing a bright red. Before Biting-Shadow-Pounces-Prey could make a move, his muscles were taken over yet again, and he was force-jumped backwards in a body twisting move right as a blinding white wall of force slammed into him.

#

Biting Shadow stirred. Every inch of his body throbbed with pain.

Do not move. I am fixing the damage.

He didn't even whine at the voice this time, it would take too much energy and the slightest movement caused sharp pains to stab him. His jumbled memory was trying to piece together what happened.

Gorel had a thermal bomb... a device that vaporized... killed both men.

Biting Shadow felt a wave of sadness, not his own.

I was Gorel's partner for a long time. We had many adventures together. The voice sighed. *It is always hard moving to a new host, but he was special. A good man. I will miss him.*

I want to go home. Those were the first man-words Biting Shadow formed. They also accompanied his more traditional means of expression which involved an image of him slinking into the den and curling up under his favorite ledge.

Give me a few more minutes and you should be able to walk again. Good thing you have heavy armor, otherwise we would both be dead.

As soon as Biting Shadow could breathe without sharp pains, he made a tentative move to stand. A little wobbly-legged, he took a couple of test steps and felt relief at the lack of pain. He slowly made his way back to the source of all his trouble, only to see nothing but a big hole in the ground.

We need to take the pod back to the spaceship and escape before Kel's men come looking for him.

The strange sphere thing was the only unusual object left standing and must be what the voice was harping about, but Biting Shadow ignored it. *I want to go home.* He turned his back on all the strangeness, cloaked, and headed for home.

Stop!

Are you going to force me? More man-words, this time laced with anger. Biting Shadow was determined to learn how to fight the frozen muscle thing.

No. I cannot do that unless your life is threatened. The voice sulked.

Biting-Shadow-Returns-Home didn't care. He had bigger problems, or rather one really big one. The pack song warned him that Fierce Mother had returned, and she was very angry. He rushed home and slunk into the den, tail tucked between his legs, and paused when his nictitating membranes retreated. Blind, he didn't dare go farther in until his eyes adjusted to the darkness. Instead, he crouched, waiting for the expected blow. But moments passed and the smell of Fierce Mother remained at a distance. Finally able to see, he looked up and saw her pacing in front of his siblings who were jammed into a tight space under his least favorite ledge. Fierce-Mother-Worried-And-Angry kept sniffing the air and her armored scales were in full attack mode. Apparently, she hadn't seen him yet.

You are a mere pup? Well, that explains many things. The voice seemed both surprised and worried.

Ignoring it, Biting Shadow kept his eyes on Fierce-Mother-Protecting-Young. Her eyes continually scanned the den, never once lingering on where he was. Normally, he'd be excited at finally avoiding her gaze, but now he just wanted to get past the punishment so he could get something to eat and sleep.

She cannot see you with my alterations. You are truly invisible along all wavelengths.

When Biting Shadow dropped his shadow form, Fierce Mother stiffened, then lunged. Startled, he sent images of him playing with his brother and sister. Too scared to even raise his defenses, he kept blasting her with memories.

I may have made a mistake. The voice was worried.

Biting Shadow was worried too, but for a different reason. Fierce-Mother-Protecting-Her-Young stood right in front of his nose with her teeth bared in a vicious snarl. She sent him a sequence of images: standing before her, tainted, smelling foreign, wrong, and danger. He sent back images of his encounter outside the den while dropping his head down to beg forgiveness. His tail wagged in entreaty and he sent an image promising to behave in the future.

Fierce-Mother-Casting-Out-Danger growled. Then her thought-images and emotions cut off abruptly, and Biting-Shadow-Asking-Forgiveness could no longer feel the pack song. For the first time in his life, he was truly frightened. When Fierce Mother snapped at his nose, Biting Shadow stumbled back, tail tucked between his legs. Confused at the loss of connection, he whined, but Fierce Mother took no pity on him and drove him out of the den. As he cowered outside in the stiffening breeze, she stood guarding the entrance. From him.

This is my fault. I did not know your shadow form was tied to your identity. I am truly sorry.

Biting Shadow gazed blankly at Fierce Mother. He could no longer read her even though he could tell from her body language that he wasn't welcome. His best guess was Fierce-Mother-Casting-Out-Not-Son which made Biting-Shadow-Outcast feel like crying. He felt worse when he realized it was no use emoting his own emotional modifier, none of his family would ever hear him now.

A strong gust of wind almost pushed Biting Shadow off his feet, interrupting his self-pity. The memory of a howling sound outside the den crystalized into an image Fierce Mother had projected once when he tried to escape, that of death if caught beyond the den at the wrong time.

We need to get to the pod. If that is destroyed, we lose our chance to...

The voice was saying man-words that Biting Shadow had no energy to deal with. He cried out once more and belly crawled a step closer to the den, but Fierce Mother snapped and snarled. Finally, Biting Shadow gave up. If he couldn't return to the only safety he knew and he didn't find shelter soon, he would die.

Go to the pod.

This time the thought was accompanied by an image of the sphere thing. Lacking any better plan, Biting Shadow ran as fast as he could, stumbling more often than not with the almost constant wind gusts. His heart was racing and he could smell his own fear even with the gale blowing everything around. This was beyond his experience. And he was all alone.

You have me. You are doing fine, keep going.

Easy for the voice to say. It wasn't getting tossed about like prey.

You can call me... Shade. The voice managed to convey a sense of distaste as he spoke the name. *And I am more than just a voice, but you are too uneducated to understand.*

The only thing Biting Shadow understood right now was the dangers of remaining exposed. *Where is it?* He could no longer see landmarks to guide him to the spot and was beginning to panic. The wind was worsening and it wouldn't take long before even his strong armored hide would be of no use.

I am working on a solution. There! Try that.

Biting Shadow wasn't surprised this time when lines showed up in his vision. This entire day had been too strange. What was one more oddity?

It's a contour map. I have added outlines to the surrounding terrain.

Once Biting Shadow adjusted to it, he saw the ridgeline where the sphere thing was located and headed that way. He crouched low to the ground to shave off some of the gust's strength.

The sphere thing, *pod*, was rocking violently back and forth.

Hurry, get up the ramp!

Biting Shadow needed no further encouragement as he scrambled up the unsteady ramp. When his nose touched the solid pod surface at the top, it parted. He flinched at the unexpected reaction but shot forward as soon as he could wedge his body through the opening. Scary strange was better than certain death any day. The opening, *door*, sealed behind, leaving him in a larger space that was rocking from side to side.

The stabilizers are failing. Quick, get to the control panel and touch it with your ... paw.

Biting Shadow blinked as his nictitating membranes retracted and looked around the odd looking space. It was perfectly smooth and spherical, unlike the den. There was a rectangular object raised in the center with a lower stepping stone behind it. Both gleamed white, a new color he was having trouble relating to. Everything so far in his world was red or black or shades of dark.

The voice blasted an image of him climbing onto the stepping stone, *chair*, to touch the tall thing, *control panel*. The pod's shaking intensified. Fear lent swiftness to Biting Shadow's limbs, and he leapt onto the chair and pawed the console in a single, fluid bound.

Lights blinked and high-pitched chirping sounds emanated from the panel. A low rumble vibrated underneath the pod, then Biting Shadow was pressed against the floor by some unseen force.

We are lifting off.

He flattened down in the chair and held on with all four claws while the room shuddered violently.

The landing pod is compensating as best it can, but I have never seen winds this strong before. Hold on.

Biting Shadow didn't know which was scarier, closing his eyes, or keeping them open while watching everything shake around him like it was about to tear apart. His stomach was doing flips in time with his racing heart. After a dive that left him nearly weightless, the pod surged upward and Biting Shadow slammed back into the chair. This time, he sunk his claws deep into the soft surface for better purchase and tried not to vomit.

After a final jolt, everything stopped.

We are safe now. I am about to dock with the spaceship. Which you have no clue about. The voice sighed its frustration. *Let me show you.*

The solid white pod walls faded to display specks of white against a blacker than black background.

This is what space looks like.

It looked terrifying. Biting Shadow wasn't used to such open space and instinctively curled tighter in the seat. His shadow flicked on, but the immense structure ahead of them, and getting larger, made him feel exposed.

That is simply the spaceship. Nothing to worry about. It is designed to travel between the stars, the specks of light.

Biting Shadow kept his fearful gaze on the large spaceship and was grateful for the soothing voice which chattered on about space and man-things. Despite wanting to be brave, he was trembling. All of this was too overwhelming. Plus he ached for Fierce Mother's comforting caresses that he would no longer experience.

The spaceship opened its mouth, *docking bay*, and swallowed their pod whole. It settled into the center of a larger room that was cluttered with what Biting Shadow assumed to be man-things.

Crates, supplies, food, medicine, tools, maintenance drones... The voice trailed off and gave a mental shrug. *Oh, very well. Like you said, man-things.*

Biting Shadow pictured the voice in physical form, complete with tail between its legs and head drooping in dejection at all its man-words being ignored.

I am not a language snob. I will have you know, I have had several less erudite partners, and we always got along.

Once again, Biting Shadow didn't understand half of what the voice was saying and didn't particularly care. He was still reeling from Fierce Mother's rejection. Plus, the large space outside of the pod was yet another foreign landscape to navigate, and he was reluctant to experience any more unpleasant surprises.

It is just a large storage room. Perfectly safe.

Of course, distraction was preferable to sitting here feeling empty. Mind made up, Biting Shadow leapt out into the room and sniffed the strange-smelling air.

Recycled air has a particular odor to it... but you do not really care about that, do you? The voice exuded guilt and sadness. *I know this is a lot to ask of you right now, but we need to get through that door straight ahead and turn left.*

For the most part he simply let the voice guide him with thought images and didn't pay attention to the unusual surroundings. He did pause when they went through another door, but after that he kept his head down. There was too much color everywhere and the light was too bright.

I will make more adjustments to your eyes soon enough so that will not be a problem anymore. It is very rare to find intelligent life around an M class sun... that is the dim, red ball in your sky. There really is not a lot of color in this ship, you are simply not used to seeing much beyond black, dark purple, and red. Allow me to give you a primer while we go.

The silver colored material is metal. No, I will not bore you with an explanation of how that is made. Do not worry. The voice flashed an image of the walls to match the color since Biting Shadow had no idea. *Anything that is blue or yellow is informational.* An image popped into his mind of a perfect rectangle outlined in yellow with blue scratches, *writing.* When he glanced up, he saw the same markings on the walls. *Do not worry, I will teach you to read later. Now, go through those doors so we can enter the cockpit. I need to see what Kel transmitted.*

Biting Shadow warily approached the doors and froze when they automatically slid open like the pod doors. He quickly jumped past in case they decided to eat him and landed in a crouch.

That will not happen. There is a sensor that knows when you have cleared the doorway. Jump up in the chair and place your paw on the circular pad, exactly how you did it in the pod.

He sure hoped the shaking wouldn't happen again like in the pod.

No danger of that while we are in orbit.

Biting Shadow did as instructed. Soon after, he curled up in a ball and fell asleep.

#

Well, I have good news and bad news. Which do you want first?

Biting Shadow yawned, sat up, and stretched. When he opened his eyes, he blinked in surprise at the lack of glare.

I adjusted your eyes so you can handle more wavelengths now without getting overwhelmed. Do not worry, I kept your night vision intact. That could be handy in the future.

The voice, *I am called Shade,* was far too cheerful. The hollow feeling hadn't subsided. It was weird feeling hurt without a physical wound. When his brother bit him, it left teeth marks and was sore for a good day. This was a dull ache somewhere inside. Or not even that exactly. He stood and shook his entire body to free it of dirt and other stuff that the wind had wedged underneath his scales.

Watch the electronics! They do not like debris.

Biting Shadow ignored Shade and began grooming.

Shade huffed his disapproval. *So. About the news. Kel made his last transmission before he traveled here, so that is the good news.*

The bad news is, the trackers will be able to find the ship because this is the closest system from the last jump point. So we need to leave right now and lead them on a false trail.

Leave? That caught Biting Shadow's attention. *No.* He pulled up a memory of his family and felt heartsick.

But they cast you out. You owe them nothing. Trust me, those trackers will obliterate your planet on the off chance they can eliminate me. You do not want to be down there when that happens.

Biting Shadow flattened his ears and growled his displeasure while sifting through the man-words to express his feelings. He finally settled on, *Stay. Protect.*

No. No. No. No. I do not think you understand. You cannot stay there and the ship definitely cannot stay here.

No. Stay. Protect he repeated, refusing to budge. He may have squabbled with his siblings, but he was always the one to kill the prey when it fought back. He was the eldest, so said Fierce Mother, and that meant he was their protector, even if he could no longer hear the pack song.

Shade mentally sighed and threw up an image of Fierce Mother shaking her head from side to side. *Let me see what this ship has for inventory. There might be a way if he stocked them...*

Images flashed across the smooth surface though Biting Shadow didn't understand what he was seeing or how they were changing.

When you pressed the pad on the console, it enabled me to use telepathy to control the interface. Sensing Biting Shadow's confusion, Shade clarified. *I am using my thoughts to control the ship.* A few more images flashed by, then the screen froze on a picture of a tube-thing.

That is a cylinder containing emissions dampening transmitters. The ship has enough to blanket your planet with a network that will trick scanners into thinking there is no life. I took the liberty of deploying it since the wind storm has finally abated. I also picked up something unusual. Look at this.

Biting Shadow saw a picture of what must be the planet surface, but in the background was the outline of a shape that was far too smooth and regular to be a natural outcropping.

I think it is a ship. But...

A shrill alarm startled Biting Shadow badly enough that he jumped straight up in the air and crash landed half out of the seat. As he scrambled to prevent an awkward spill, Shade began mentally shouting. *A Quarian battleship has entered the planetary system and is headed right for us!* He shifted through displays faster than Biting Shadow could register. *I set the ship's cloaking shield, but they may have already detected us! How are they even here? They must have a base nearby. Think. Think. What would Kel do? I know!* He would document the incident and report it to Command no matter the cost. Shade's panic was tempered slightly by a sudden dose of inspiration. The screen froze on a blank page but symbols began rapidly filling it up. *Well, this text transmission will explain why he was in this system. Kel made the jump to follow Gorel. Gorel jumped again. Kel was about to follow, but discovered signs of a possible enemy base. Only a close friend would know that Kel's obsession with Gorel means he would never stop even though he could be charged with treason. It is the perfect cover story to protect your planet.* A few moments later and he resumed shouting. *Black hole's sucking singularity!*

Biting Shadow crouched, armor out, expecting something to jump at them.

Sorry. That was a curse Gorel was fond of using. The signal is being jammed. They know we are here. Look, we need to get this information to the Imperial Command. I may hate the empire, but I am still its protector. With the Quarian this close, they could be ready to invade.

Shade's protective instincts were as strong as Biting Shadow's were for his family. He could respect that. *What can we do?*

Do you trust me?

He thought of the encounter with the bomb and how Shade kept him from dying. *I trust you.*

Hang on to your seat.

Biting Shadow dug his claws in right as an invisible force shoved him hard into the cushioned back.

I am hoping we can take them by surprise and get outside of their jamming range before they overtake us. But just in case, I also have a Plan B.

A plan which involved going down into the deeper down place, *storage hold*, to grab circular objects, *bombs*, climb up a regularly spaced sequence of ledges, *stairs*, and put them in the pod. Oh, and do that as fast as possible because time was running out. At least the invisible force pushing him around was gone.

The inertial dampers kicked in. Before you head back to the cockpit, go through this door on the left.

Biting Shadow was getting tired of being told what to do, but he went through the door anyway. He stopped in the middle of a completely empty room and wondered what he was doing there. Only the walls were unusual with uniformly shaped rectangles sitting on top of one another starting at the bottom and running all the way to the top of the enclosed space.

Those rectangles are storage compartments. Shade transmitted an image showing a drawer on the lower right. He also showed a paw pushing on it, and it opening up to reveal row upon row of silvery packets.

Biting Shadow followed the instructions and grabbed one.

Good, now tear into it and eat the contents. You will need the energy. Or rather, I will need you to have the energy for what is to come.

The smell alone wafting out of the ripped packet was enough to turn Biting Shadow's stomach. The actual flavor was worse than the jellied area inside Bitey Thing that he insisted on trying despite Fierce Mother's warning.

The ship shuddered and another shrill alarm sounded.

We are being fired upon! Quick, back to the cockpit.

Shade's scream made Biting Shadow wince. His own fear propelled him down the corridor. This time, he wasted no time jumping into the chair, only to sit there feeling useless. He hated that. Give him prey to bite into and he'd be fine. Not being able to see the enemy or do something about it was terrifying.

Here. Let me bring up the visuals.

An ugly box-like rectangle with odd spines was growing larger on the display.

They are closer than I expected. Time for Plan C.

That sounded ominous. Biting Shadow dug into what little was left of the chair cushion as the ship began veering side to side.

I set the automated defenses. Now if we can only make it to that small moon ahead.

The screen split into two images with the round object on the left half, and the ship chasing them on the right.

Shade emitted a brief wave of sadness. *I really wish Gorel was here. He was the expert at harebrained schemes. He would definitely appreciate this plan.*

The ship shook again. *What is that?* Biting Shadow thought as a red light began flashing on and off.

We are losing shield strength. One more direct hit and... never mind, we made it. And... now!

The ship lurched to the side and a jarring vibration set Biting Shadow on edge.

That was the landing pod taking off with full burn to make it look like we are trying to escape. Not exactly recommended procedure while on a moving ship, but it makes us look desperate and unarmed.

Biting Shadow watched as the small pod shot away from their ship. The enemy shifted course to intercept. Shade vibrated with glee as the pod was swallowed up.

It actually worked!

Before Biting Shadow could ask what was going on, a bright light turned the entire display white. *What happened?*

Hang on. Their ship is only crippled. We need to take it out. Shade set a course to slingshot around the moon and went full throttle.

Biting Shadow watched nervously as they approached the drifting ship from the rear. This was a lot like how he pounced on prey. But they weren't slowing down.

I need you to close your eyes and think of a safe spot back home. Make it as real as you can with the way it smells, looks, feels, sounds, and tastes.

Why?

There is no time, just do it!

Shade's panic made it harder for Biting Shadow to do as he asked. One last glance at the display showed the enemy ship taking up the entire display. Petrified, Biting Shadow squeezed his eyes shut and pictured his favorite ledge in the den. It was a tight space which rubbed up against his scaly hide and smelled of stone and moist dirt. The sound of water dripping in the right corner always soothed him to sleep and had an earthy flavor. For a second he could actually feel himself wedged under the cool slab before pain split his head into pieces and an overwhelming weakness sucked him into darkness.

#

Shade barely had enough energy to keep the pup's invisibility shield from falling. The only reason it hadn't fallen yet was because of how instinctive it was for the young pup, even unconscious, to activate it when frightened. Judging from the alert and angry adult female growling not five feet away, he was almost certain that dropping the shield would result in death.

That was not his only worry. Most adults had trouble handling jumps, let alone a young pup with a smaller body mass that had less energy to draw upon. *Please stay alive, kid. I do not want to be responsible for your death.* It was bad enough he took a host without permission, let alone a child host. He scrambled to do what he could to bolster the pup's weakening systems, and for a moment it was a close thing. Then, remarkably, the pup began recovering with a speed unlike any other host he had experienced or read about. Yet, there was something familiar about his current host's genetic makeup. Almost like he had encountered this species before. But with his impeccable memory, he would never forget. Unless it was in his distant past when everything was erased... Now that was a troubling thought. Shade set aside further speculation and settled in to wait for his charge to wake up.

#

It was hard for Shade to believe three months had passed without once leaving the planet. For an entity with perpetual wanderlust that was a record. But the time was well spent teaching the young pup about basic technology. The kid was eager to learn once he got past the fiasco of being cut off from his pack. Shade still regretted his mistake, even if it would make leaving easier. For leave they must. Three months was too long to hold onto vital information. The Quarian could already be invading. It was more than time to get back, especially since his host had matured into one of the strongest teleporters he had ever seen. He also had another reason...

Biting Shadow began to stir.

Shade slapped a shield around his innermost thoughts. Now was not the right moment to bring that up. Once his charge was fully conscious, he broached the unpleasant subject. *Well, I have good news and bad news. Which do you want first?*

Not this again. I'm not even awake. Biting Shadow stood up and stretched, emphasizing his point.

The good news is you are as trained as I can make you without practical experience. The bad news is, we need to leave. I cannot wait any longer to deliver the message.

One last visit, Biting Shadow demanded, followed by a wave of sorrow.

Of course, Shade agreed, vastly relieved that his charge had not argued against it. In the blink of an eye, they were standing on a small promontory looking down at a medium sized cave. Three young pups were playing right inside the entrance. Biting Shadow's sister, Small One, sat outside, watching over them. Of course, that was not her real name now that she had reached adulthood. But without the pack song, they had no way of knowing what she changed it to. One more reason he felt guilty. Biting Shadow had already checked on his mother and brother yesterday, so this was the final goodbye. Shade could feel the waves of sadness coming from Biting Shadow. They matched his own feelings about his previous host, Gorel. They would both do well with some action to distract them from their grief.

Biting Shadow gave a small whine. *I'm ready.*

With barely a pop, they teleported.

#

Sad-One-Misses-Brother looked away from her pups to the ledge above and somehow sensed deep down that her outcast brother was truly gone this time. Despite the broken pack song, she always sensed when he visited and now she regretted not greeting him. She whined and tried to picture him staying safe, but she knew he was seeking trouble. It was in his nature. Well, if he ever returned, she'd reject the pack's decision and greet him properly. For he might be changed beyond recognition, but he was still her brother.

-o-

C. Gold is an avid World of Warcraft gamer and book reading junkie. When she's not reading about wizards or spaceships, she's writing stories about them. She currently has a short story and first novel published in her Darklight Universe fantasy series. Biting

Shadow is an introduction to her other work in progress - a science fiction series based on a once powerful peace keeping organization that kept the galaxy safe. With them overthrown, and an evil emperor in charge, the galaxy is in big trouble.

Homepage: **http://www.thegoldenelm.org**
Mailing List: **http://www.thegoldenelm.org/newsletter**

Gate of Dreams

by Rick Partlow

Andre Damiani stood at the center of an inside-out world and pondered the vagaries of the gods. Their handiwork surrounded him, an endless landscape of mechanisms that seemed more sculpture than machinery; liquid, flowing curves and vague, hazy edges that made him wonder if they were real or some ViR fantasy.

There was gravity in the inside-out world, pulling toward the interior surface of the hollowed-out asteroid, just one of the miracles of the gods humans had come to call the Predecessors. The gravity was there, but its source eluded his best engineers in much the way that the Predecessors themselves eluded him. They were always a few centimeters out of reach, just like the tantalizing shapes of the long-abandoned asteroid base, close enough to touch but incorporeal as a dream.

"I hate this place." The ViR analog of Gene Wycoff appeared beside him in a cloak of purple flame, a frown marring his otherwise perfect face. You could always tell the *nouveau riche*... their Virtual Reality representations were idealized, with flashy clothes and flawless features. Damiani's own icon was identical to its real-life counterpart, dressed in a dark business suit, a practice he'd learned from his father, along with many others less benevolent. "I always feel like something's watching me."

"Me too," Damiani said, eyes flitting back to the mind-warping interior of the asteroid. "I love it." He fixed Wycoff's analog with a business-like stare. "Tell me you've found something."

The researcher smirked with satisfaction. "This base, the Centauri Belt outpost and the original find in the Solar asteroid belt are lined up like an arrow... pointing here." He stretched out an upturned palm and a star system sprang to life above it... more grandstanding, Damiani thought. "Some Federation scout stumbled onto it during the war." Eight planets began to spin with exaggerated speed around the G-class star. "He wouldn't have taken much notice except that readings indicated the second planet out was habitable." The view zoomed in to a lush, green, moonless world a bit smaller than Earth. "He called it Avalon."

"Do we have anyone there?"

"As a matter of fact, we do," Wycoff informed him. "There's a load of iridium in the equatorial mountains and we've had a mining unit there for over three months. Apparently, they've been having some trouble with squatters, so a Security team is also on its way out."

"Damn," Damiani hissed. That would complicate things. "But no one has found any sign of Predecessor activity?"

"Not yet." Wycoff shook his head, perfect hair whipping about artfully. "But if I were you, I'd hurry..."

#

Damiani's stomach lurched as his transport came out of Transition Space and the verdant beauty of Avalon filled the cabin's main viewscreen. Down there, he thought with a certainty that surprised him, were the answers for which he'd been searching.

"Sir," a voice buzzed in the cabin's intercom. "Message from Chief Investigator Wellesley of the Corporate Security Force."

"Yes?" he muttered, annoyed that she already knew he was here.

"She requests," the word stank of euphemism, "that you meet with her at your soonest possible convenience."

"Where is she now?"

"She's in a Squatter village at the foot of the central mountain range on the planet's largest continent," the pilot told him, "but she's right in the middle of something. She says you should meet her back at her field office."

"My time is valuable," Damiani informed him. *Just as valuable as hers*, he added to himself. "Take me down outside the village. Now."

"Yes sir."

One of the other, less pleasant lessons his father had taught him was to recognize potential adversaries early... and keep them off balance.

#

"Citizen Mitchell," Trina Wellesley sternly intoned. "You and your... followers will not be allowed to interfere with Corporate Council matters. I strongly urge you to leave this area or your lives will be in danger."

Caleb Mitchell watched her with an air of quiet amusement, hands clasped serenely in front of him. They were a study in contrasts, he and the Corporate Security Force agent. Every aspect of her appearance was sculpted by an artificial intelligence program to reflect perfection and resolve without losing her feminine core. She was the embodiment of professionalism in a vat-grown business suit, surrounded by a half-dozen CSF troopers in grey body-armor, their pulse carbines held at the ready.

Mitchell and the handful of men and women with him had the look of eighteenth century tenant farmers in home-spun clothes of local fiber and animal hides. Mitchell himself was an impressive man, not overly tall but dense and well-muscled in a way that his loose tunic and pants couldn't totally disguise. His hair was an unruly red mane and a long beard flowed down over his chest in a collage of Viking chieftain and Biblical patriarch.

"Agent Wellesley," he replied. "If we allow you to bring your plasma miners in, our lives are over. We could move to the other side of the planet, but that will not save us *or* our home from the radioactive wastes that your machines will produce."

"Those mining machines *are* coming up this mountain tomorrow," Wellesley declared, her tone shrill with impatience. "No one invited you and your squatters to settle here, and no one is going to bend over backwards to accommodate you. If you don't take advantage of our offer of transport *now* and vacate this area, you'll die."

"Our lives are transitory," Mitchell's voice grew harder, his face more grim. "The life of this planet is not. Living worlds are precious jewels to be cherished and preserved, not to be carelessly fouled. We cannot allow it."

"*You* can't allow it?" Wellesley exploded. She took a step forward and the muzzles of the troopers' lasers swung around to back her up. "I'll be the one deciding whether *I* allow you to live..."

Before she could finish the threat, a scream of rocket engines ripped apart the sky and a wedge-shaped shuttlecraft descended on incandescent columns of fusion-heated air only a hundred meters away down the hill. A wave of sweltering heat washed over the gathered Corporates and squatters, sending three of the armored Security troopers to their knees and driving the others backward. All except Mitchell. He remained motionless, eyeing the landing spacecraft stolidly, a Jesus regarding the storm. So he was the only one to see when the shuttle's boarding ramp slowly extended and Andre Damiani disembarked, a jaunt to his step, a hint of a smirk on his face.

Andre watched Investigator Wellesley pick herself off the ground and imagined he could see the steam coming off her. Most men would have at least attempted to *look* contrite, but Damiani strode into the midst of the group as if he were walking into a party held in his honor.

"Ms. Wellesley," he nodded to the CSF Investigator.

"Damiani," Wellesley hissed, "I was so *hoping* your reputation was overstated."

"I believe you requested my immediate presence," he cocked an eyebrow. "From your tone, I *assumed* it was urgent." He glanced at Mitchell and his ragged entourage. "Problems with the locals?"

"We don't have any problems here, Mr. Damiani, and I plan to keep it that way." Wellesley was in his face with one step, her voice lowering to a threatening rasp inaudible to the others. "I know all about you and your obsession with the Predecessors, Golden Boy. You may have conned those doddering fools on the Executive Board with your fantasies of finding caches of lost technology, but you've yet to produce a single usable device. I've had my eye on you for a long time."

"Gosh, Agent Wellesley," Damiani said, intentionally loud. "I *am* flattered, but it's my personal policy not to get romantically involved with co-workers." He smiled broadly. "Maybe we can still be friends."

Wellesley's eyes flared with anger and for a moment Damiani thought he had pushed it a centimeter too far, but then she took a deep breath and stepped back from him.

"All right. If that's how you want it." Her tone was chillingly dismissive. "But you'd better not make a mistake, Damiani. You may think the worst that can happen to you is to lose your seat on the Council, but I can assure you that will be the least of your problems if you cross me."

Wellesley stalked off toward her groundcar, followed after a moment's hesitation by her guard escort, leaving Damiani standing alone with the squatters. He looked Mitchell up and down, sensing somehow that there was more to the man than met the eye.

"Mr. Damiani," Mitchell said without preamble, "I believe I know what you are looking for. And I can help you find it."

Andre stared at him, taken aback.

"And just what might I be looking for, Mr. Mitchell?" he finally asked.

"You *think* you're looking for the secrets of the Predecessors," Mitchell delivered the answer that froze Damiani's blood in his veins, "but what you really seek is both far simpler and yet far more difficult to obtain. You seek meaning, Mr. Damiani." Mitchell's gaze burned into him with the intensity of an exploding star. "Meaning for your aimless, meaningless life."

Damiani wanted to laugh at him, wanted to offer some witty comment about their clothes and make a grand exit back to his shuttle. But something stopped him. *Surely not his religious ramblings*, part of Damiani's mind protested. *I can't be that far gone! No, it must be the Predecessors... If there's the chance he might know anything...*

"All right," Andre shrugged. "What's the hook? What do I have to do?"

"Our village is three kilometers west of here," Mitchell gestured up the mountain. "Meet me there in twelve hours. Alone."

Without waiting for an answer, Mitchell turned and led his group back up the path, quickly disappearing into the thick, tangled foliage.

Andre watched them go, shaking his head in amazement. For the first time in his life, he was at a loss for words.

#

Caleb Mitchell stared silently at the night sky, at a field of stars so close it seemed he could reach through the thin, mountain air and touch them.

"Some people look at the stars," he said, "and think how insignificant we are... individuals, humans, life in general. Just blades of grass adrift in the ocean." He turned back to Andre, who squatted cross-legged next to the communal fire at the center of the small village. "Is that what you think, Mr. Damiani?"

"Not really," Andre shrugged, tossing a wood chip into the fire. It was true...he could never think of himself as insignificant.

"What I think when I look at the stars, Mr. Damiani," Mitchell went on as if Andre had not said anything, "is how lucky this universe is to have us to appreciate it."

"That's an interesting way of thinking, Mr. Mitchell," Damiani admitted. He stood, looking the man in the eye. "Or should I say, 'Captain Mitchell?' Would you prefer that?"

"Captain Mitchell is dead," the big man declared, not betraying any surprise at Damiani's revelation.

"That's what the military records say, too," Damiani agreed. "Which, I suppose, is why Wellesley hasn't found out who you are yet."

"You don't know who I am, Mr. Damiani," Mitchell shook his head. "You only know who I was."

"Who you were and what you are, Captain Mitchell, is one of the deadliest human beings that ever lived." This time, Mitchell did show a reaction; he looked up sharply at Damiani, but swiftly buried his surprise behind a mask of complacency. Damiani knew he was taking a chance. He was alone with the man, not even any of the other squatters to witness if Mitchell decided to snap his neck. And he knew the man was capable of doing just that.

"If military intelligence found out you knew about Omega Group," Mitchell commented quietly, "they would most likely have you killed on general principles."

Damiani chuckled. "The military? Do try to keep up, Captain Mitchell. The Council has the military in its back pocket. Without us, they wouldn't exist. *We* kept them in business once the War with the Tahni was over, letting them fight our battles with the smugglers and the pirates in exchange for continued funding. If I turned you in, they would line up to kiss my ass." He shrugged. "I mean, after all, the intelligence boys probably didn't take too kindly to losing such a valuable... asset. Particularly one into which they had sunk several million credits worth of physical augmentation."

"Tell me, Mr. Damiani, why do you feel the need to use coercion when I have already said I would give you exactly what you want?"

"Let's just say," Andre shrugged, "that I am uncomfortable with the concept of philanthropy. I would rather know *why* someone is helping me, and I would rather it were in their best interest to do so."

"Fine." Mitchell smiled with an apparent sense of ease that disturbed Andre. "Then let's assume that your ploy succeeded and I am shaking with fear. Now will you allow me to help you?"

"As long as 'helping me' involves telling me where the Predecessor outpost in this system is located," Andre replied, "and not giving me your own personal psychoanalysis of whatever 'meaning' you may believe me to be seeking."

"I can take you to the Predecessors," Mitchell declared with a matter-of-factness that made it believable.

"You know where they are," Damiani said, more statement than question. "We can take my ship."

"No need for a ship. The Predecessor base is inside this mountain."

"*What?*" Andre stared at him. "That's impossible. No Predecessor outpost has ever been found on a habitable planet. It's as if they avoided them, avoided disturbing the life on them."

"All except one. *The* one. Have you ever heard of the Gate of Dreams, Mr. Damiani?"

Damiani barked out a laugh, shaking his head in amusement. "Oh, Captain Mitchell, you really had me going! I can't believe I actually took you seriously for a moment. That Gate of Dreams nonsense has been bouncing around human space for a hundred years!"

"Trust me when I say it has been around much, much longer than that." Mitchell smiled softly.

"Oh yeah, I forgot the story," Damiani chuckled. "The Predecessors had become so advanced that they grew tired of corporeal existence and decided to go through the Gate of Dreams, a relic from another reality, and become gods. I had a girlfriend once who bought into that crap." He tried to remember her name, but it slipped his mind and he hadn't thought enough of her to save his memories of her in his headcomp.

"All legends become myths with constant retelling, Mr. Damiani," Mitchell told him. "And this one has been told and retold since before humans discovered the wheel."

"But *you* happen to know the truth of it, eh?"

"There's one way to find out. If you will go with me in the morning, I'll take you to the Predecessors. There is just one problem, however."

"Of course there is," Damiani sighed.

"The problem is," Mitchell continued, "that as of tomorrow morning, this mountain won't *be* here anymore."

"The plasma miners come up the hill tomorrow," Damiani realized. He looked hard into Mitchell's eyes, wishing he could see through them into the man's cryptic thoughts. "You understand the risk you're asking me to take."

"I ask nothing of you, Mr. Damiani," Mitchell corrected him. "I only offer an opportunity. Taking advantage of it is up to you."

Andre wanted to turn and leave the man, to get in his ship and go back to his comfortable office and never look back. But something stopped him, some small part of him that wanted to believe. In the end he could only ask, "Where and when?"

"I'll find you, Mr. Damiani," Mitchell replied, then turned and disappeared into one of the huts without another word.

Damiani started down the path to the Corporate camp at the foot of the mountain but hesitated for a moment, looking up at the stars. He hoped Mitchell was right about his significance to the universe, because if he went through with this, he was going to need all the friends he could get.

#

Damiani looked from the stunner in his hand to the motionless form of the CSF guard at his feet and briefly wondered if he had finally gone over the edge. Many had predicted it, to be sure, over the last ten years, as he had pursued every angle that even had a chance to lead to the Predecessors.

Oh well, he thought, shoving the stunner into his belt, *might as well go all the way.*

He dragged the fallen guard into the shadows then quickly clambered up the ladder into the cockpit of the titanic plasma miner. Three stories tall and weighing over a hundred tons, the machine was little more than a mobile fusion reactor. It used the superhot plasma its reactor produced to vaporize rock and then sucked it through filters to separate out the valuable ores. The three miners parked in the clearing were enough to bring the whole mountain down in less than a week.

Damiani hacked the control panel's coded safeguards with a cryptography AI module he had brought from his ship, then powered the machine up. Plasma-driven turbines came alive with an otherworldly shriek that tore at his nerves. He had never operated one of these things before, but what he had in mind required little in the way of finesse and much in the way of brute force. He glanced at the horizon and saw a hint of false dawn... not much time.

Recalling the operations manual he had hastily downloaded after leaving the mountain village, Damiani shifted the miner into forward and opened the throttle halfway. The machine lurched forward as massive twin tracks received a sudden jolt of power and he struggled with the steering yoke to keep his course straight towards the side of the second miner. Pulling as close to the other machine as he could, he hit the controls to open the plasma ports to their lowest setting. The shielding on the fusion reactor opened the barest of cracks, less than a millimeter, but the cockpit's canopy filters went black to protect him against the fires of the sun brought down to man.

Damiani slammed the port shut with a slap of his hand on the control lever, and when he backed his machine away, he saw with some gratification that the miner he had targetted no longer had a portside track; instead, there was a lump of molten and running metal settling into a small crater in the ground.

Wrestling his machine on a course for the third plasma miner, Damiani found himself hoping that the stunned guard had been far enough away to avoid a fatal dose of radiation from his use of the plasma port.

That's odd, he mused. He hadn't thought of anyone but himself in quite a while. *Mom would be so proud*, he snorted.

Cracking the plasma port once more, he melted the side of the third mining machine to slag, then powered his miner down and slipped out of his seat, ducking down beneath the control panel. Drawing on the schematics he had read, he opened an electronics maintenance hatch and yanked out a pair of relay boards, slipping them into his jacket pocket. The boards could be replaced, but they would have to be programmed to interface with the miner's AI, and that would take at least a day's work, enough time for what he had to do.

Andre was climbing down from the cab when something hard and unyielding slammed between his shoulder blades, sending him sprawling to the ground, his back spasming in agony. Forcing his eyes open against the pain, he found himself looking up at the visored helmet and yawning pulse-carbine beam emitter of one of the CSF troopers.

"Don't move or you're fried," the man shouted, his voice muffled slightly by his helmet.

Damiani's hand was positioned over his stunner and he was about to make a grab for it when a dark blur slammed into the guard and he went down in a heap. The dark blur materialized into the form of Caleb Mitchell, his hand extended to help Damiani to his feet.

"I said I would find you," the man reminded him, smiling thinly. "Quickly, there's not much time."

Still dazed by Mitchell's sudden appearance, Andre nodded wordlessly and followed the man back up the mountain trail at a brisk trot.

"Once those guards come to and identify me," Andre gasped out, struggling to keep up with Mitchell, "I'm a dead man."

"Oh?" The ex-commando glanced back at him, not the least bit winded. "And you think you were truly alive before?"

Before Andre could snap back a reply, Mitchell turned back and picked up the pace and Andre suddenly needed all his breath for running. Lacking night vision equipment, Andre had to stick close to Mitchell and trust the infrared filters implanted in the man's eyes as they made their way up the rough trail.

Damiani expected hordes of CSF troopers to dog their heels, but he heard nothing except the hard stomp of his own footsteps as the local primary edged its way over the horizon. He tried to spot the path to the squatter village but he soon realized they were taking another trail, rougher than the one he had traversed last night, and leading much higher up the mountain. Rocks and vegetation yanked at his ankles, determined to trip him up with every step, but Mitchell refused to slow his pace, doggedly trotting up the ever-steeper slope.

Andre ordered his implanted pharmacy organ to dose his system with endorphins and adrenaline in an effort to keep up with the fast-moving Mitchell. His thoughts grew fevered as his conscious mind battled the fight-or-flight response to the biochemicals, and abject terror battled with a building excitement at the prospect that he might actually find the Holy Grail for which he had been seeking all these years.

And then what? A little voice asked, so small and still, yet heard clearly through the mists of his overloaded brain.

The question almost made him halt in his tracks. What *would* he do once he had found the secret of the Predecessors? Would the Corporate Council be so grateful they would forgive all his sins, or would Wellesley simply have him killed and take the credit for herself?

"Halt where you are or we will open fire!" The amplified voice startled him so badly he nearly lost his footing and went tumbling off the side of the trail, but he managed to catch himself in time. Twisting around, he saw the flattened oval of a CSF flyer floating a hundred meters above them, its ducted fans nearly silent, the gaping muzzles of its twin grenade cannons pointed his way.

Andre raised his hands in surrender. No more worries about what he would do when he found the secrets of the Predecessors, anyway... he would never get the chance. Then he felt himself yanked violently backward by the material of his tunic and the lights abruptly went out.

It took him a moment to realize that he was still alive, and a moment longer to figure out that he had been pulled inside some sort of cave. He rolled to a crouch and felt in his pockets for a flashlight.

"Don't bother," Mitchell's voice came from somewhere behind him. The man uttered a word in a language never meant to be spoken by human vocal cords and suddenly the passage was flooded with light.

Andre looked around, trying to spot the entrance they had used, but saw nothing. In fact, he was in the *middle* of a long, narrow corridor, its walls glowing with an interior light. "Where in the hell am I?" He breathed, his voice thick with disbelief.

"Exactly where you wanted to be," Mitchell told him, striding off down the corridor.

"What about the CSF goons? It won't take them long to figure out where we went."

"Do *you* know where we went?"

Damiani considered that for a moment before shaking his head in consternation and following Mitchell. The corridor gradually widened into a hall, the walls curving up into a barrel vault lit from within. When he stared at those walls, Andre thought he could begin to make out images within them, ghosts of a dead race watching him with detached amusement.

"I have a story to tell you, Mr. Damiani," Mitchell spoke as they walked. "It's a story that predates not only the existence of humanity but the very existence of this *universe*. But first you will need a brief lesson in physics. Everyone knows that this universe originated from the expansion of a singularity... the sort of rend in the fabric of spacetime that is at the center of a black hole. What everyone is not aware of is that *every* singularity, every black hole in this universe, is the placenta of a baby universe, just as we are living on the inside of a singularity, so are those singularities the outside of other universes."

"I've heard this theory," Damiani told him. "But as far as I know it's unprovable, just mathematical speculation at this point."

"*We* haven't proven it," Mitchell corrected him. "But it is the truth. Universes produce offspring, just like any other living thing, and just as in any other example of natural selection, some are more successful than others. Some physicists have speculated that this explains our existence, that the physical conditions which are ripe for producing black holes, and the baby universes within, are also those which are prime for producing life. But this is not so. Only a minute fraction of the universes produced by this birth process have conditions that are right for life, and the development of life in a naturally occurring universe is miraculously rare. Which brings us to the story I have to tell."

They turned down one last corridor, one so long Andre couldn't see the end.

"So long ago that the very concept of time has no meaning, a life bearing universe developed by chance, and in this universe evolved a race of beings which managed to survive the pitfalls of intelligence and develop a technology that makes ours seem as the stone tools of the *Homo Habilis* by comparison. This race realized what a tragedy it was that so few universes gave birth to life, to intelligence, and they sought a manner to make this right. They needed a tool to grow universes which would not only contain intelligence but which would *be* intelligent, be complex enough to actually be considered a living thing.

"For a hundred thousand years they tried to build this tool, beginning with simple mechanisms for creating black holes out of existing stars, but they lacked any sort of control, any way of assuring that the universe they were creating would bear the fruits of life. Until finally, they stumbled upon the key, and built a... device, I suppose, though the word is hardly adequate."

"The Gate of Dreams," Damiani mumbled with a sort of shocked acceptance. He wasn't sure what shocked him more, Mitchell's story or the fact that he believed it.

"This device imposed a pattern upon the created universe, a living pattern drawn directly from the brain patterns of sentient creatures. It did have one drawback, however, but one that was unavoidable. To impose this pattern on the new universe required an act of will, one that could only be achieved by a living being. One living, sentient being must sacrifice its corporeal existence for every universe created."

Andre stopped in his tracks and stared at Mitchell.

"And they did this voluntarily?"

"Are you saying you don't think it's a good trade?" Mitchell asked with some amusement, pausing in his pace but not turning back.

Andre ran after him, thoughts churning at the idea of giving up his life to become a god.

"You're saying they all did this?" He asked breathlessly. "They all sacrificed themselves to create new universes?"

Ahead of them, Andre began to see a strange glimmer, like the sun reflected off the ocean.

"Every one of them," Mitchell confirmed. "Once it had started, there was no way to stop it. They stopped reproducing, waited till their children had matured enough to make the decision on their own, and then, as a species, committed themselves to this course."

"Hold on a second, if they created the Gate of Dreams in their universe, how did it wind up in this one?"

The shimmer became a strobe of gentle light as the edges of the doorway became clearer.

"The Gate is not a physical object, though it seems as one," Mitchell explained. "Rather, it is a wormhole through the fabric not only of this spacetime but in *all* spacetimes, and in the very nothingness that underlies it all. It has been given form by a twisting of hyperdimensional physics that makes our Transition drive seem pale by comparison. It exists, in different forms, in every universe that has sentient life... and it has a way of finding those individuals and those species which will use it."

"So the Predecessors..."

"Used it. The last of the Predecessors went through the Gate a thousand years ago."

Damiani felt himself physically deflate. Somehow, he had always held out the hope he would actually *meet* the Predecessors face to face, ask them all the questions that had dogged him since his youth. Yet somehow that seemed incredibly naive, given that what Mitchell was saying was true. The Predecessors were nothing but the latest in a chain of predecessors that led back not to the distant past of this galaxy but beyond the reach of spacetime itself to another *universe*. And for once in his life, he felt small and insignificant.

Damiani fell into a subdued silence as they finally reached the end of the corridor, passing through into a chamber so huge he was halfway convinced it couldn't fit under the mountain. Its walls were polished crystal, shimmering in reflection of the object at the center. But for that, the massive chamber was empty, as if anything else would detract from the silent grandeur of the Gate.

For that was what it surely was, Damiani thought. There was a... discontinuity in space somewhere at the center of the chamber. Exactly where was hard to pinpoint, as the whole effect seemed unreal, like a phantom glimpsed from the corner of the eye. There were colors in the discontinuity, colors that shouldn't have been visible to the human eye but somehow were. It gave the impression of a ring shape, and though Damiani couldn't seem to perceive the center of the ring, by looking away and then quickly glancing at it, he caught the hint of something... absent.

"Why did you bring me here?" he asked. "Am I supposed to go into that *thing* like the Predecessors did?"

"You say 'supposed to' as if you had some overarching destiny, Mr. Damiani," Mitchell chuckled. "None of us have any fate other than that we assign ourselves. You could, indeed, step through the gate and become the god of your own private universe, if that is what you think would fulfill you. Of course, you would be the last being in this universe to do so."

"The last?" He frowned. "What do you mean?"

"When those mining machines are repaired, your colleague Ms. Wellesley will level this mountain. This installation and everything in it will be buried beneath tons of slag, and no one will ever set foot on this world again."

"You have all this..." Damiani waved a hand demonstratively. "Can't you stop them?"

"Of course I could. Through brute force, and at the price of revealing this place's existence to the government and the Corporate Council."

"Same difference," Damiani mumbled.

"Quite." Mitchell smiled thinly. "Eventually it would come to war, and I would be given the choice of killing to protect this place dedicated to life, or letting it fall into the hands of those who might destroy it out of fear and ignorance."

Andre regarded him silently for a moment. Here were the secrets of the universe, hell, of *all* universes, laid out in front of him. Here was the key to his destiny, the one way for him to be as important as he felt he deserved to be. The opportunity to be a god. Who gave a damn what happened after that? He opened his mouth to say as much, but it wouldn't come out. What came out of his mouth instead, to his great surprise, was: "What can I do?"

What was even more surprising, he meant it.

#

"Has there been any sign of him?" Trina Wellesley asked tightly, staring at the command vehicle's sensor screen.

"Nothing since..." The security officer trailed off, not wanting to bring up the report of Andre Damiani disappearing into the side of a mountain. It had become a sore point with Wellesley.

"Well, he can damn well *stay* hidden in those goddamned mountains for all the good it will do him," the Corporate Investigator snorted dismissively. "By tomorrow afternoon, the plasma miners will be online and that mountain will be a heap of slag."

"I doubled the guard around the repair crews," the security man assured her. "Just as you ordered."

"It's probably a waste of time," she shook her head, stepping out of the open side door of the vehicle and into a night lit almost to day by the searchlights of the gathered vehicles. All around were bustling security troops, eager to look busy to escape the wrath of Investigator Wellesley, which had assumed prodigious dimensions since the debacle with the plasma miners. "He would be a fool to come back here."

"Ma'am!" one of the security officers exclaimed, looking up from a monitoring station. "We have a transmission going through the orbital comsat! It's from Damiani!"

"Who would he be calling?" She frowned.

"Council Headquarters on Earth, Ma'am," the officer answered.

"Jam it!"

"Too late, Ma'am," the man shook his head. "He's using a priority code, and by the time we overrode it, the message would already be gone."

"What the hell does he think the Council can do for him now?" Wellesley wondered, staring into the night.

"It's not what they can do for me," came a voice from somewhere behind her, "but what I can do for them."

Wellesley whipped around, followed closely by a pair of spotlights and the muzzles of a score of pulse carbines. Standing there like an apparition in the midst of their camp was Andre Damiani, carrying a rock in one hand and something about the size of a suitcase in the other.

"One of you morons grab him!" Wellesley shouted, spurring half a dozen of the CSF troopers into motion.

"I wouldn't do that," Damiani cautioned, but the security troops kept coming... until the first of them got within ten meters of him.

The CSF officer dropped face-first to the ground like a pleasure doll with its circuits blown and the others skidded to an awkward halt, glancing back at Wellesley.

"What did you do to him?" she asked, eyes widening.

"The same thing I could do to you if you don't behave," Damiani told her with not a trace of the self-satisfied smirk that would have accompanied that warning just twenty-four hours ago.

One of the CSF guards whispered a curse and jerked the trigger of her pulse carbine. Fifty quick-discharge superconductor coils overloaded at once, blowing apart the gun's magazine in a shower of sparks and throwing the trooper backward head over heels. She jerked spasmodically, smoke pouring from her hands and chest where the electrical energy had seared the soft armor of her uniform.

"It would be best," Andre confided, "if none of you tried that again."

"All right, Damiani," Wellesley hissed. "You've made your point. I don't know how you're doing this, but you've got all the cards. What do you want?"

"First off, you'd better get her some medical attention," he motioned toward the trooper who had tried to shoot him. "She's going to die in a couple of minutes unless you get her heart going again."

Wellesley looked at him strangely for a moment before nodding to the chief security officer. He grabbed a medical kit from the command vehicle and ran over to the fallen woman.

"As for what I want," Damiani went on, setting the dull grey case on the ground, "that's simple." He slapped a palm against a barely-visible plate on the side of the case and it began to silently unfold like a blooming rose, its metallic petals gleaming with an interior light. "What I want is to give you what *you* want, Agent Wellesley."

He gently placed the rock in the center of the device, then stepped back a pace. The light from the segments of the machine intensified slowly but inexorably, forming a perfect hemisphere around the center. It grew so bright it outshone the searchlights yet somehow none of them could look away from it. And then, as quick as an eyeblink, it faded and in the center of the thing was a glowing ingot of pure ore that all of them could recognize by sight.

"Gaia's Blood," Trina Wellesley breathed. "Is that what... I mean, it can't be..."

"It's pure iridium," Damiani assured her. "You can test it. If you think I'm conning you, you give me something to put on there, but whatever it is, this thing will turn it into pure iridium. Or pure platinum... or whatever you want."

"That's Predecessor tech," Wellesley declared. "You found a cache of it here, didn't you?"

He nodded confirmation. "And this is just the handy, portable model. How would you like a matter transmuter the size of a warehouse?" He grinned. "No more plasma miners, no more habitable planets contaminated, no more expensive and inefficient prospecting. Hell, I'll bet you could even make this puppy turn out antimatter."

Wellesley looked him in the eye and knew he had won. The transmission to the Council was undoubtedly a report claiming credit for the find, an end run around any attempt by her to hijack it. With a sigh of resignation, she slumped against the side of the command vehicle. "I suppose they'll give you a seat on the Executive Board for this."

"A seat?" He smiled broadly at her. "I was thinking something more substantial than that."

Wellesley swallowed hard at the thought and fell silent.

Andre strolled through the assembled vehicles, away from their beaming spotlights and into the open meadow. He glanced up at the mountain, a hint of envy in his heart. Somewhere up there, Mitchell and the others were taking their turn at godhood. His own journey through the Gate of Dreams would have to wait, for the mantle of guardian had fallen upon him. He would see to it that the Gate remained intact and accessible to those who were called, until someday someone came to take his place. And in the interim, he would dole out enough technology to keep the Council from tearing the planet apart... and perhaps enough to destabilize their stranglehold on the government.

Andre looked up at the stars, remembering what Mitchell had said. How lucky this universe was to have us to appreciate it. But not just *this* universe...

-o-

Rick Partlow is a former US Army Infantry officer who graduated Florida Southern College with a History degree. He's published thirteen SF novels in four different series and is working on the fourteenth. He currently lives in central Florida.

Homepage: **https://rickpartlow.com**
Mailing List: **http://www.facebook.com/dutyhonorplanet**

The Following Star

by Elizabeth Baxter

"Let's play fetch!" said Dog, his back end waggling from side to side in excitement.

Angus pulled a shiny red ball from his pocket and held it above Dog's head. "Reckon you can fetch this?"

"You bet I can!" Dog went down on his front paws, fluffy yellow tail swishing.

Angus pulled his arm back and hurled the ball as hard as he could. In the low gravity, the ball sailed out, hit the metal wall, and went soaring out of sight down the corridor. Dog, yipping like an excited puppy, bounced after it, looking ridiculous with his lolloping, low-grav steps.

Nurse would be annoyed at Angus for messing with the gravity again, but low gravity made fetch so much more *fun*. Besides, it wasn't Angus's fault if his classes had been cancelled was it? The asteroid belt they were navigating demanded all of Nurse's attention, so Dog hadn't been able to download today's lesson from her memory. Angus and Dog needed something else to keep them occupied. They'd come up with Fetch.

Angus pulled himself along the corridor, trying to keep up with

Dog. Down here on the lower decks, the corridors felt eerie, as though he walked through a forbidden world. Nurse had cut the electrics, so the only illumination came from the Following Star, bathing everything in glittering silver light.

Dog was scrabbling around by the door to the stasis room, desperately trying to snaffle the ball, which kept bobbing out of reach. Finally, he gave up. He snapped his jaws shut and plucked the ball out of the air with his paw.

"Got it!" he said triumphantly.

"Not fair! You cheated!"

Dog put his paws on his hips. "I cheated? You turned the gravity down!"

Angus shrugged.

"Throw it again!"

"In a minute." Angus pulled himself over to the stasis room door and peered through the window. Nurse didn't like him going near stasis. Nurse said it was unhealthy the way he'd stand there and stare but Angus couldn't help himself. All the other passengers aboard ship were inside that room, only a few meters beyond the thick walls.

Angus had spent hours at this door, staring in. Which pods belonged to his parents? His grandparents? Would they even recognize him when they reached the new home world?

Angus had been six when the colonists went into stasis. He didn't remember much from back then. When he thought about it, his mind went foggy. Fractured images of hospital beds, monitors, and his mom's voice promising to take him somewhere to get better. Then he woke up aboard the ship with Nurse and Dog.

Now he was ten. When they reached the home world would Nan still ruffle his hair like she used to? Would Da still carry him on his shoulders? Or would Angus be too big? Angus's breath misted the window and he wiped it away irritably.

"We can't risk any damage to the stasis pods," Nurse would say if she saw him now. "You know how valuable they are."

Of course Angus knew. He could be trusted! He was ten years old!

Dog floated over and nudged the ball towards Angus. Dog's tongue hung out the side of his mouth and his nose had turned bright pink like it always did when he was excited. It was some glitch in his program that Nurse had never quite got round to fixing.

Dog's bushy eyebrows pulled into a frown. "What's up? You daydreaming again?"

Angus didn't answer.

Dog sighed. His shape began to melt. He morphed into Boy, about the same age and height as Angus but with blond hair and pale skin.

"We'll do something else instead," said Boy. "Anything you want. We'll go in sim and play some football. What d'you think?"

Angus didn't want to play football. He wanted to see his parents. But it was no good telling Boy such things. He wasn't a real boy, any more than Dog was a real dog, so how could he understand how Angus felt?

The com panel on the wall suddenly crackled into life. "Angus? Have you been meddling with the gravity again?" Nurse sounded annoyed.

"Only on this deck." Angus said quickly. "And I'll fix it, promise"

"You'd better. Go and have a wash. Dinner is in half an hour."

#

When Angus and Boy reached the bridge, they found Nurse staring at the view screen. The Following Star filled the screen, a big ball of silver that always trailed them. Her rose bud lips curled into a smile when she saw Angus.

"There you are!" She swept across the room and enveloped Angus in a tight hug. As usual, Angus noticed her odd, metallic smell. Nurse hugged him for a long time as though it had been ages since she'd seen him last, and not just since breakfast.

"Let me look at you," she said at last, pushing Angus back to allow her to appraise him from top to bottom. Nurse had put on the pink suit she saved for special occasions. "We've done it, Angus," she said. "We've made it through the asteroid field."

A little bubble of excitement swelled in Angus's stomach. "You mean?"

"Yes! There's nothing in our path now except empty space! We'll reach the new home world in no time!"

A tumble of thoughts and images flashed through Angus's head: faces, voices, places he'd seen as a child. "When will we arrive?"

"Oh, in about two years."

The bubble of excitement popped. Two years? He couldn't wait that long!

"Come along," Nurse said. "Dinner's ready. I hope you've washed your hands."

Nurse had set up a circular dining table, covered in a white tablecloth. The table looked weird surrounded by all the computers and screens and stuff.

Nurse pulled out a chair and daintily perched herself on the end. Angus took the seat which faced the view screen. He always chose this spot. From here, he could watch the Following Star while he ate.

Nurse said the Following Star was their guardian, seeing them safely to the new colony. The Following Star had always been there, never catching them and never getting further away. Angus wondered what would happen when they reached the colony. Would the Following Star catch them up at last or would it continue past them into deep space?

"Angus?"

Nurse held out his plate, which she'd piled high with sausages and mashed potato. Angus took the plate, careful not to spill gravy on the pristine white tablecloth. Nurse could be funny about things like that.

"So, tell me about your day, little one," Nurse said.

"Didn't do much," Angus answered.

"Except playing with the gravity on the lower decks," Nurse said, frowning. "What about his studies?" This was addressed to Boy.

Boy had been busy shoveling food into his mouth as if he was starving. Boy always ate like that and it annoyed Nurse no end. Angus wondered why she'd programed him with habits which bugged her so much.

"We've been using the laser sensors to map our trajectory," Boy said with his mouth full. "And Angus managed to use the robot arms to take some dust samples yesterday. We'll analyze them tomorrow."

Nurse tousled Angus's hair. "Ah, my clever boy. I knew I was right to wake you. The colonists are lucky you're their chronicler."

Angus grunted noncommittally. When he was little he'd felt proud that Nurse had chosen him to record their journey. She could have chosen anyone in stasis, but she'd picked him. He knew it was a great honor. He knew it was a great responsibility and that he would hold a unique place in their new society. How many times had

Nurse told him how special he was? But now loneliness had devoured any pride he'd once felt.

Choose someone else! He wanted to shout. *Put me into stasis! I'm sick of being special!*

But he didn't. He ate silently.

"Look at you," Nurse said. "You've gotten gravy all down your shirt." She leaned over with a napkin and began dabbing at Angus's front. Angus suffered it in silence. Why did she treat him like a little kid? Didn't she know he was ten?

"I want to go into the stasis room," he announced suddenly.

Nurse sighed. "I'm getting a little tired of this, Angus. Why must you try my patience? Don't you think I have enough to do?"

Angus's cheeks grew hot with shame. But with anger too. "I won't do any damage! I won't even touch the pods. I just want to see my parents!" Angus knew his voice had turned into the high-pitched wail of a child.

Nurse threw the napkin onto the table and rested both hands on her lap. Her eyes had changed from blue to violet, a sure sign of her fury. Boy morphed into Dog and slunk under the table, tail tucked between his legs.

"I don't impose many rules on you, Angus," Nurse said. "Far fewer than I should. But this rule is non-negotiable. It's my duty to keep the colonists safe until we get home. I hoped by now you would understand that. You will stay away from the stasis room. You will not endanger my passengers."

Angus looked at the Following Star and back to Nurse's pale, angry face. He burst into tears. Huge, runny-nosed sobs shook his body. Nurse folded her strong arms around him and pulled him close.

"Everything will be all right, little one. Promise me you will leave the stasis room alone. Can you do that for me?"

"Y... Yes. I... I... promise," said Angus. He buried his face in Nurse's shoulder and cried till his throat hurt.

#

Angus crept up to the bookcase. He moved carefully, trying to make sure the old floorboards didn't creak. A bulge in the curtain gave away Boy's position. Angus smiled. When he got up close, he lunged forward, grabbed the curtain and shouted, "Found you!"

Boy shrieked and jumped out of his hiding place. "What did you do that for? You scared me!"

"Well, you should choose a better hiding place shouldn't you?"

"I bet you only found me coz you cheated!"

They were in sim, a recreation of an old house back on Earth. The house had loads of nooks and crannies, great for playing hide-and-seek. Boy was rubbish at this game, perfect for what Angus had planned.

"Your turn to be it," Angus said.

Boy scowled, folding his arms across his chest. He screwed his eyes up tight and began counting loudly. Angus waved his hand about in front of Boy's face to make sure he wasn't peeking, and then ran down the hall. As soon as he turned a corner out of Boy's line of sight, he opened the door and tumbled out into the corridor. This left Boy in sim and hopefully unaware that Angus had crept out.

Angus blew out his cheeks and ran his hand through his hair. Nurse would be really angry if she found out what he was up to. She'd be disappointed in him too, which was worse.

But it's her fault! Angus told himself.

But you promised! A voice answered in his head.

I don't care!

Screwing up his courage, Angus trotted down the corridor. Soon he found himself traversing the silent lower decks where the only light came from the Following Star. He felt like a ghost walking these empty places. He arrived at the stasis room and took a small rectangular disk from his pocket.

The little red access light kept flashing on the door of the stasis room. Angus held out the rectangular disk. It was a sim pad that Dog had used in Angus's lessons weeks ago. Dog had programed the pad to simulate an emergency, in this scenario, a power drain. Whilst Dog had been using the program to teach Angus emergency procedures, an idea had come to Angus. It was a crazy idea. It would never work. But it was all he had.

Angus wiped his sweaty palms on his pant leg and pushed the sim pad into the slot on the door panel. It connected with a satisfying little 'click'. Something beeped and the yellow light on the sim pad began to flash, indicating that the sim had started uploading its program to the computer system. Angus looked down the corridor one way, and then the other. All clear. Boy must still be in sim and

Nurse hadn't yet detected this unauthorized upload.

Minutes dragged by. Angus shifted from foot to foot, expecting alarms to start going off any minute. He didn't even know if he was doing this right. He hoped the simulated emergency program would trick the computer into thinking the emergency was real so it would give Angus access to the override.

"Hurry up!" Angus pleaded, wringing his hands.

"What are you doing?"

Angus spun around to see Boy standing at the end of the corridor, a puzzled frown wrinkling his pale forehead.

Angus shrugged nonchalantly. "Nothing."

Boy looked from Angus to the sim pad, to the door, to Angus again. "You're trying to break into stasis!"

Panic brought Angus to the edge of tears. "So what if I am? It's not fair! I just want to see them, that's all!"

Boy winced, and then glanced around as if frightened of being overheard. He walked cautiously towards Angus. Half way down the corridor, he morphed into Dog, and looked up at Angus with his huge, liquid eyes. "Don't go in there. Please."

"Why shouldn't I?"

"It's not safe."

"I don't believe you! What's in there that's so bad?"

Dog crouched down, looking dejected and fearful. He'd tucked his tail between his legs. "Don't make her angry. Please."

Angus hesitated. He'd never seen Dog look like this. Why was he so afraid of Nurse?

Then he realized. Nurse would blame Dog for Angus's behavior because Dog was supposed to take care of him. Dog was Angus's friend. Angus didn't want him to suffer because of his own behavior.

Angus grabbed the sim pad and wrenched it out of the door slot. Angus folded onto his knees, put his arm round Dog's shoulders and pressed his face into the soft yellow fur.

"I'm sorry, Dog. I'm sorry."

#

Angus sat at the dinner table, desperately trying to act as if everything was normal, as if he hadn't disobeyed Nurse or tried to break into stasis. He was sure Nurse could see straight through him. She'd been irritable all evening, griping about creases in Angus's clothes, slopping out the meal with uncharacteristic aggression. She'd pinned her hair into an intricate bun and the half-moon spectacles resting on her nose made her look austere and unapproachable.

Angus had tried engaging her in conversation. Nurse normally loved to hear about Angus's day: what he'd learned in class, what he'd been doing in sim. Not today. Today she just smiled and said, "That's nice, little one," as though her mind was on something else.

She knows, Angus thought. *She knows and she's going to punish me!*

They ate in silence. Angus tried to finish his food but he didn't have an appetite. Dog wasn't faring much better. He'd remained as Dog rather than morphing into Boy like he normally did at dinner – a sure sign of his own nerves. Dog picked at his food as though it might be poisoned.

Angus risked a glance at Nurse. She was staring at the view screen. Her red-painted nails made a loud clicking noise as she drummed them on the table. The Following Star filled the view screen. Nothing new there. What had caught Nurse's attention so much?

Hang on, Angus thought, leaning forward for a better look. *Is the Following Star bigger?* But surely that couldn't be possible. In all the years they had been traveling, the Following Star had never changed. It had remained exactly the same distance away, exactly the same size on the view screen, at exactly the same level of brightness.

It's definitely bigger. And looks brighter too.

"Is… is everything all right, Nurse?" Angus asked.

Nurse turned to him. A tiny vein kept throbbing in her temple. "Everything is fine. Eat your dinner."

Angus glanced at Dog who gave a tiny shrug. Angus skewered a piece of broccoli on his fork and began eating again.

"We have to change course," Nurse said.

Angus nearly choked on his broccoli. "Why? I thought we were on a straight course for the new home world."

"So did I. I was wrong."

Angus paused. "Is this because of the Following Star?"

Nurse's eyes narrowed. "What do you mean?"

"It seems closer. Is it catching us up?"

Nurse lurched to her feet, knocking a cup of water over. "Why must you ask so many questions, Angus? Don't you trust me? Haven't I always looked after you? Done what's right for you?" Two spots of color had appeared on her cheeks and a strand of hair had come free of her bun, bouncing around her face.

"I'm sorry," Angus spluttered. From the corner of his eye he saw Dog slide from his seat and creep towards the door.

"Dinner is over," Nurse announced. "Dog!"

Dog froze, looked over his shoulder guiltily. "Yes, Nurse?"

"Take Angus back to his quarters. He is not to leave them again until his lessons tomorrow. And no sim time for the next two days. Is that clear?"

"Yes, Nurse."

Is she angry because I tried to break into stasis? Angus thought. *Or is she angry because I asked about the Following Star?*

He pushed back his seat and followed Dog out the door.

#

"Just here," said Dog, pointing to a spot on the rotating holographic globe, "is the area that's been designated as our landing spot. Nice and flat with a clean water source and mineral deposits in the hills."

Angus studied the globe. He and Dog were in the science lab and Dog had programmed a sim of their new home world. It was blue mainly, with thin pockets of land bunched around the equator. Angus wondered if it had rivers and trees, and all the hazy things he remembered from Earth.

"The ship will be our home for the first few years," Dog said. "Until we get the dwellings sorted out."

A sudden thought struck Angus. "What will you and Nurse do?"

Dog frowned. "What do you mean?"

"You and Nurse can't leave the ship, so what will you do when we go?"

Dog's frown deepened. "I... I'm not sure."

Angus patted him on the shoulder. "Don't worry, Dog. We'll find a way to take you with us. I promise."

Dog lolled his tongue out in a smile then held up a paw. "So, question: how will we convert the new world's solar energy to electricity?"

Angus opened his mouth to speak but the ship suddenly lurched and Angus stumbled forward into the console.

"What was that?"

"Must be the new course change," Dog replied, studying the readout. "Things will settle down in a minute."

But they didn't. The floor began shaking violently. Somewhere nearby, an alarm shrieked. Angus glanced at Dog, hoping for reassurance, but Dog's ears were pressed flat and he'd tucked his tail between his legs. Angus's heart began to race. What was happening? Had Nurse lost control of the ship? Were they under attack?

"We've got to get to the bridge. Come on!" Without waiting to see if Dog followed, Angus sprinted for the door.

In the corridor, some of the ceiling panels had come down, revealing exposed wiring that fizzed and gave off showers of sparks. Angus shielded his head with his arms and ducked under it.

Angus had no idea what he'd expected to find when they reached the bridge: the room in disarray, Nurse battling to keep the ship under control or something. He hadn't expected to find the room untouched, and Nurse staring at the view screen as she always did.

"Is everything all right, little one?"

Angus skidded to a halt on the shiny metal floor. The ship was still juddering. Couldn't Nurse feel it? On the view screen, the Following Star seemed bigger than ever.

"I was worried." Angus managed at last.

Nurse knelt down so her eyes were level with his. "Worried, little one?"

"The ship feels funny."

"Oh that," Nurse said, straightening. "Nothing to worry about. We are going a bit faster, that's all. We'll get to the home world quicker. It's what you want isn't it?"

Angus nodded. He walked over to the view screen. The Following Star was definitely closer. And now he saw an outline within it, a shape he couldn't quite identify. He placed his hands on the console. The pilot would sit here, if the ship had a human crew. When he was little, Nurse would let him pretend to fly the ship. Angus suddenly saw that the readouts had gone crazy. Warning lights were flashing all over the console.

"Why are we going so fast?"

Nurse raised an eyebrow. "I've told you why."

Angus looked at the Following Star then at the warning lights on the console. "I don't believe you!" he blurted. "It's because of the

Following Star isn't it? It's going to catch us!"
Color leaked out of Nurse's face. "Angus, I am starting to lose
my patience with you. Go back to your room."
"I won't! Not until you tell me what's going on! I'm not stupid! I
know we are going too fast! You are tearing the ship apart!"
"Enough!" Nurse's eyes blazed. Little sparks of light danced in
them. She took three steps towards Angus. "You will not question
me! Go to your room. Now!"
Mouth hanging slack with fear, Angus ran for the door. He passed
Dog who was cowering in a corner.
"Dog!" Nurse shrieked. "You will stay and help me!"
Angus tumbled out into the corridor and ran, not knowing where
his feet were leading him. The ship was shuddering as though being
battered by heavy winds. Angus struggled to keep his feet. He was
more frightened than he'd ever been. He'd never seen Nurse like
that. She looked like she might kill him.
He jammed his fist in his pocket to keep it from shaking. His
hand brushed something rectangular. Of course! The sim pad. He'd
kept it with him ever since he'd tried to break into stasis.
Angus halted, leaning on a wall to keep his balance. For a second
he panicked, all thoughts fleeing. But then a decision came to him.
Angus approached the stasis chamber hesitantly. The light from
the Following Star had become so bright that the metal walls
gleamed, making Angus squint. He felt so frightened he thought he
might be sick. Frightened of Nurse. Frightened of the Following
Star. But most of all he was frightened that he wouldn't be able to
break into the stasis chamber. And even if he did? Would he
recognize his parents? Or would they seem like strangers?
He took the sim pad from his pocket and pushed it into the slot in
the stasis chamber door. The yellow upload light began flashing.
Minutes ticked by. How long would it take? Minutes? Hours?
A beep, and the light on the sim pad flashed from yellow to green.
A message suddenly appeared on the sim pad: *Please enter override
code.* Angus punched in the six-digit number that he'd seen Dog
entering in sim.
The door slid open.
Angus stood there. His heart thumped so hard, it felt like his ribs
might crack. This was it. The room opened out in front of him like
some forbidden garden.
Angus stepped inside. A wide aisle stretched the length of the

oblong room. On either side of this aisle, rows of black stasis pods marched into the distance. The air smelled weird, kind of metallic, like Nurse. And it was cold. Very cold. Some of the pods were rimed with ice.

All these people, Angus thought, *and I've never seen any of them.*

Almost shyly, Angus moved over to the closest pod. Ice covered the window. Angus scraped it away with his sleeve. Then he raised himself up onto his tiptoes and peeked inside.

The pod was empty.

Angus's breath caught in his throat. *Don't be stupid!* He told himself. *It doesn't matter if one is empty.*

Angus crept up to the next pod and peered through the window.

Empty.

Angus took a shaky breath and moved onto the next one. The same. Empty. Panic clawed up Angus's throat.

Desperately, he ran from one pod to the next, peering into each one, hoping to find someone. Anyone.

But they were all empty.

He reached the wall and stood staring at it blankly. Nowhere else to go. Nowhere left to look. He was alone. He'd always been alone.

Angus crumpled to his knees and sat hunched over, arms wrapped protectively around himself. He squeezed his eyes tight shut. Perhaps if he closed his eyes he could pretend…

"Hello? Can anyone hear me?"

Angus's head shot up.

"Is anyone there? Please respond."

The voice echoed oddly as though it came through a lot of static. Angus climbed to his feet.

"This is *Sungazer.* Please respond."

The voice came from the control desk by the door. Angus edged towards it.

"Can anyone hear me?"

"H…hello?" Angus said.

"Who's that?" The voice sounded male.

"My name is Angus."

There was silence for a long time. Angus began to think he'd imagined the voice. The con crackled and a new voice spoke. "Angus? Angus, is that really you?"

This voice sounded female, excited or frightened or maybe both. "My baby! It's you, isn't it?"

THE FOLLOWING STAR   97

Angus backed away.

The man spoke. "Quiet. You're frightening him. Angus, listen to me. My name is Thomas Fulford, captain of *Sungazer*. We've been trying to contact your ship for a long time. Why haven't you answered our hails?"

"What hails?" Angus said, bewildered by the authority in the voice. "I haven't heard any hails!"

"And your Pilot program? Why has it not responded?"

"There isn't a pilot. Nurse flies the ship."

Silence. When the voice spoke again, it was slow and deliberate as though the speaker was thinking through each word. "Who is aboard the ship, Angus?"

"Just me and Nurse and Dog."

"Only the Nurse and Companion programs are running? What about Pilot? Navigator? Physician? Tech?"

Tears were gathering in Angus's eyes again. "I've never heard of them!"

The voice spoke soothingly. "It's all right, Angus. There's no need to be frightened."

The woman's voice cut in. "It's not all right! Don't tell him that! Listen to me, Angus. We can't catch you. You must shut off the engines so we can catch up. Can you do that?"

Angus shook his head. "But you're not real! You're just a voice! Why should I believe you?"

"I am real, Angus, I promise." The voice sounded desperate now, frightened. "Tell him Thomas. Tell him!"

The man's voice spoke again. "Angus, you are ten now aren't you? I need you to be very grown up. The truth is, you shouldn't be out here. The Nurse program malfunctioned. You were ill, but getting better. When we tried to take her offline, she went crazy, snatched you and launched the ship. But we had no idea she was piloting without the proper programs. Jeez, it's a miracle you've survived this long. Angus, you have to disable the ship. Let us catch up and take you home."

Angus looked around at the empty stasis pods. Nurse had lied to him. He'd lived his whole life feeling lonely. He'd hoped that loneliness would end someday. But it wouldn't. Not if he stayed with Nurse. He didn't know if he could trust the voices on the con. But he had to take a chance.

"What do I have to do?"

#

Angus trotted through the ship's corridors. He chanted a string of numbers over and over in his head. Everything seemed dream-like. He kept expecting to wake up any moment.

But the ship was still shaking. It had become so bad that rivets had come loose and the walls were cracking. So Angus kept moving, running the numbers over in his mind so he wouldn't forget.

He paused at the bridge. Pulling in a shaky breath, he opened the door and walked in. He noticed the Following Star before anything else. It had grown so big that it filled the entire view screen and lit the bridge with blinding white light. And it didn't look like a star anymore; it looked like a ship with its hull lights blaring. Angus stared.

"Little one?" Nurse was wearing a flowing blue dress that highlighted her eyes. "Have you come to apologize?"

With difficulty, Angus tore his eyes away from the view screen. Had the voices come from there? From that other ship?

"I'm sorry, Nurse. I didn't mean to upset you. Can we be friends again?"

A smile lit Nurse's face, making her seem altogether human and younger. She bent down and threw her arms wide, allowing Angus to run into her tight embrace. "Of course we can be friends again," she whispered as she pressed her mouth against his ear. "But you must promise me you will stop being naughty."

"I promise."

"Good boy," Nurse said, ruffling Angus's hair. "Now run along to your lessons. Dog may go with you."

"Can't I stay here with you?" Angus put on his most innocent expression.

Nurse cocked her head as she looked at him. The request seemed to please her. "Of course, little one."

Angus trotted over to where Dog was busy punching commands into a console. Dog glanced at Angus with wide, fear-filled eyes.

Nurse turned back to the view screen and Dog whispered, "I know where you've been, Angus. The alarm sounded on this console the second you broke into stasis. I only just managed to stop Nurse from noticing it. How could you be so stupid?"

Angus shook his head but not to deny Dog's accusation. "Did you know?"

"Know what?"

"That the stasis chamber was empty."

Dog looked away, his eyebrows pulling down. That was answer enough.

Angus thought of the numbers Captain Fulford had told him, making sure he had them right. At best, he'd have about twenty seconds before Nurse detected him. He had to get this right first time. Heart racing, he began tapping the numbers into the console.

"What are you doing?" demanded Dog.

Angus didn't answer. A hot ball of panic pulsed in his belly. His hand shook violently. He had entered half the numbers now. Ten more seconds needed.

"Stop it!" cried Dog. "Are you mad?"

Yeah, probably. But I don't care!

"Little one! What are you doing?" Nurse demanded suddenly.

Angus flinched. But he carried on punching in the numbers. Only three more to go. Two more. One.

A stinging, backhanded slap flung him onto his back. He landed so hard he cracked his head on the floor and lay there, stunned.

Nurse loomed over him. "I asked you a question," she said in a hard, cold voice. "What have you done?"

Angus wasn't sure if he'd done anything. He wasn't even sure if he'd managed to enter the last number before Nurse hit him. Then Angus noticed something. The ship had stopped shaking.

Nurse whirled away, disappearing from his view. Rolling onto his side, Angus saw her standing at the console. Her hand had attached itself to the console by lots of little tendrils. Her eyes had gone completely white, like she was blind. After a moment, she ripped her hand away.

"You've disabled the engines!" she screeched, bending over Angus once more. "How?"

Angus moved his mouth but didn't have enough breath to answer. Nurse reached down with one hand and yanked him to his feet. She pulled his face close to her own. "Answer me!"

Angus's head wobbled about on his neck but he was too dazed to speak.

With a cry of fury, Nurse threw him across the bridge. He sailed through the air and crashed into the far wall where he crumpled to the floor. Pain exploded through his body. Blood flooded his mouth.

He tried to raise his head but couldn't.

"How could you betray me like this? Haven't I brought you up well? Haven't I always cared for you? Loved you?" Nurse advanced towards him, face contorted with fury.

Then suddenly Dog was there, standing in Nurse's path. His lips pulled back in a snarl, hackles raised along his back. "Leave him alone!"

"Get out of my way, Dog."

Dog shook his head.

Something hissed off to Angus's left and the bridge door suddenly slid open. Angus struggled to make sense of what he saw. People. Standing in the doorway. But that couldn't be right. Could it?

Dog reacted first. He bounded towards them, "Get Angus! I'll hold her off!"

Then he began snapping at Nurse's heels, pulling at the hem of her dress with his teeth. Nurse shrieked, aiming savage kicks in Dog's direction.

Angus's vision dimmed. A voice said by his ear, "You are going to be all right, Angus. We've got you." Then he felt like he was being lifted and the racket of Nurse and Dog's fight faded into the distance.

#

Angus woke in a soft bed with a white cover pulled up to his chin. To his left a monitor beeped and some sort of drip was attached to his arm. A dull pain still throbbed in his head. A face hovered into view above him: a woman with short dark hair.

"Angus?"

Angus moved his tongue around in his mouth, working up enough saliva to speak. "Where am I?"

The woman laid a cool hand against Angus's forehead. "On *Sungazer*. In sickbay. Do you recognize me, Angus?" She sounded slightly desperate.

Angus began to shake his head. He'd never seen this woman before. But then he hesitated. That voice. And the way her eyes crinkled up when she talked.

"Mom?"

Tears filled the woman's eyes. "My baby. I've got you back."

Angus remained silent for a long time. Was this a dream? Were he and Dog in sim? But the woman seemed very real.

"The Following Star," Angus said at last. "It was you?"

She nodded, stroking a hand through his hair. "We've been following for over three years. I had almost given up hope of ever catching you."

"What about Nurse and Dog?" Angus asked. They were all the family he'd ever known.

"We can't override the Nurse program. I'm afraid the ship will be lost." She nodded towards the window.

Angus turned to look. Nurse's ship was drifting off to starboard. It looked utterly lifeless, dead. Angus climbed out of bed, despite his mom's protests, and pressed his face against the window. Dog was on that ship. His only friend. He hoped to see a yellow face looking out of one of the portholes but there was nothing. Tears leaked from the corners of Angus's eyes. Despite his mom sitting there, he'd never felt so lonely.

Something smacked into his shoulder. Turning, he saw a red ball on the floor by his feet.

"Let's play fetch!"

Angus looked up to see a familiar yellow face grinning at him.

"But…but…" Angus stammered.

His mom smiled. "We managed to transfer your Companion program."

"Come on, Angus, let's play fetch!"

Angus threw his arms around the furry yellow body and held it tight. Tears dribbled down his chin and dripped onto the floor.

"Good dog," he whispered. "Good dog."

-o-

Elizabeth Baxter grew up in the heart of England and makes her home on the edge of the Peak District where the brooding landscapes fuel her imagination. When not writing she enjoys reading, hiking, and cramming as much world travel as she can into one lifetime. She's been writing since she was six years old and plans to continue for as long as she's able to hold a pen or tap away at a keyboard.

Homepage: **https://elizabethbaxterbooks.com**
Mailing List: **https://www.subscribepage.com/e1f2r4**

The Renewal

by Zen DiPietro

Arlen Stinth had always had a nose for business. When she was five and all the other five-year-olds had imaginary tea parties, Arlen sold imaginary cookies at a substantial profit.

On her planet, this was a highly exciting trait for a child to have. When Rescan parents suspected business sense in their child, they immediately began telling their friends that he or she had 'the nose'. More often than not, this proved to be a false alarm and the child in question would go on to be a doctor or an engineer or a teacher. But not so with Arlen. She had the nose early, and she followed it right out into space, going into business as soon as she was old enough to make legally binding contracts.

Traders were the rockstars of Rescissitan. Arlen knew how odd the people from other planets found that fact. She found it equally as odd that people who worked as entertainers were the admired ones on some planets. Entertainers didn't risk their lives to get a freighter of highly reactive chemical agents to its destination. Entertainers stayed on the ground, going around in circles, doing their song and dance like a dog pleading for a treat.

"Traders know how to live." She leaned back into the pilot's chair of her ship, which she'd named the *Stinth,* and clasped her hands over her stomach.

She'd just made a tidy profit on some surplus anti-grav units. They'd cost her next to nothing besides the time to transport them. The money she'd made would cover her fuel for the next few weeks.

Her ship wasn't beautiful, and she was well aware that people sometimes mistook it for a ripper's vessel. But no one hated rippers more than Arlen. She was no cheat, and she didn't endanger lives. She abided by all PAC regulations, and her customers knew they could trust her word. Rippers gave Rescan traders a bad name, and were the reason there were so many stereotypes about her people.

She hoped to someday overhaul her ship's exterior, but for the time being, she was satisfied with her ride. Its outward appearance didn't reflect how efficient her engines were, or how many cubics she'd put into ensuring all its other systems worked flawlessly. The *Stinth* was a beauty in every way except for looks.

She sat forward, remembering that she should check in with Cabot. He'd never admit it, but she knew he worried when she went too long without checking in. Several months prior, when he was little more than an acquaintance, he'd handled a dicey situation for her. It had involved some contraband and a highly volatile situation. Though she'd been innocent of any wrongdoing, Cabot Layne hadn't had any reason to get involved with her problem. Yet he had, and he'd become a dear friend. Her best friend, actually, though he was old enough to be her dad. She suspected he saw himself as a sort of father figure to her.

She was about to open a channel on the voicecom when she noticed a strange sensor reading. Something was streaking through this solar system at an impossible speed. She felt a hot knife of worry in her stomach. Her ship must have a sensor malfunction, and that could be a harbinger of terrible things. She was days away from any possible assistance.

Checking over her systems eased her concern. She found no other anomalies. Though she and her ship didn't seem to be at risk, she wouldn't be satisfied until a qualified engineer gave her beloved ship a clean bill of health.

Scrap.

Strange thing about that sensor malfunction, though. It maintained its velocity on a direct vector. Just as a ship would.

Sensor blips didn't do that.

With no other viable theories, Arlen was forced to accept that something was actually moving at an unnatural, intergalactic speed. It had to be a ship. One from another galaxy, capable of insane speed. Certainly, no one in this galaxy had that kind of technology. The galaxies didn't mix much, due to the tremendous travel time between them. Mostly they stayed in contact via long range communication, and every so often, ships passed from the edge of one galaxy to the fringe of the next.

The rate of speed she was looking at could definitely change all that.

Should she try to make contact? On one hand, it was an exciting idea. Who would have thought she'd ever be in the position of making first contact with a species previously unknown to her galaxy? She would gain a massive amount of cred in the trader community and beyond. It would put her on the map as someone to watch in the business world.

On the other hand, such a gigantic unknown was contradictory to her nature and her profession. Sure, some risks reaped great rewards, but this situation didn't seem likely to be of that variety.

She watched the ship travel into near-instantaneous communications range on a perpendicular vector, and she had a sensation of terrible isolation. Usually, she loved her spacefaring independence, but as she watched the vessel streak across her sensors, she felt very lonely to be the sole witness.

She should tell someone, to warn them or something. But who would she tell? Who would even believe her?

"I wonder if I can get some data with a passive scan." She often spoke aloud when doing a solo trading run. Otherwise, she might go weeks without using her voice, and that was weirder than talking to herself.

"What material can handle that kind of stress?" she muttered as she tried to get a reading. Just a tiny bit of such an advanced substance would sell for a fortune. Any information she could glean would also be worth something.

But no luck. Either the thing was going too fast, or her ship's computer just had no idea what it was seeing. Or both.

Briefly, the *Stinth's* coordinates shared relative points on the x and the y axis, separated only by the distance of the z axis. Then the moment of parity ended, and the ship continued along the x axis.

Arlen felt relief along with a touch of disappointment. No one would ever believe this. If she tried to tell anyone, they'd chalk it up to either space fatigue or a trader's tall tale, designed to entertain as well as exaggerate feats of business acumen.

She squinted at the sensors when they showed the ship slowing down and altering course on a wide arc. Even at the reduced speed, it took a very long distance for the ship to swoop around.

Coming directly at her.

"Oh, scrap," she muttered.

#

She'd been fascinated by the alien ship, but now she was terrified. There was no reason for it to make such a sudden change in direction except that it had noticed her and wanted to make contact.

Possibly violent contact.

There was no point in trying to outrun it, and Arlen wasn't the kind of trader who played bad odds. The die had been cast, so she sat and waited to see what came up.

A blinking light indicated a communication request. At least they were asking to talk instead of blasting her into space dust. She decided to be cautiously optimistic.

She opened a channel. "This is Arlen Stinth of the *Stinth.*" She loved saying that. It never got old. "Can I offer assistance?"

Not that she could possibly offer anything these people would need. She probably seemed like a historical anachronism to them. Or a lower species of life, maybe.

The voicecom transmitted a voice, but Arlen didn't understand a word it said. Clearly, these people didn't speak standard, and she sure didn't speak their language. This could be a problem.

The voice spoke again. It was unlike anything she'd ever heard. It sounded like a language of all vowel sounds.

"I'm sorry, I don't understand," she answered.

After a pause, the voice spoke again. It seemed to be asking a question.

"I still don't understand."

A longer pause ensued. Was this first contact situation to be nothing but a missed opportunity? Maybe these people would just decide communication was impossible and move on.

She no longer felt afraid. Her fascination with the situation and the idea of a new species of people had taken over. Damn her curiosity. It got her into trouble sometimes.

"Understand now?" the voice asked.

"Yes! Yes, I understood that." Her excitement grew.

"Translation circuit working. Improvement with more speak."

"Um, okay. What should I speak about?" She'd already identified herself, though perhaps they hadn't understood her then. "My name is Arlen Stinth."

"Greetings, Arlen Stinth. Our name is Evekenderpar."

Our name? Was she speaking to multiple people who shared a clan name? Or did the alien mean that their kind were the Evekenderpar? The only hope of finding out was continuing to speak.

"I'm pleased to meet you. Your ship is unfamiliar to me. It seems you've come a long distance."

"Yes, long distance. Exploration interrupted by murder. Fast away."

That sounded bad.

"Is everyone on board your vessel okay? Do you need medical assistance?"

"The renewal occurs as scheduled. Food for the emergence must needs."

The words went together, more or less, but the meaning eluded Arlen. "I don't understand."

"Food." Then the voice said something unintelligible. An image appeared on her voicecom.

"That's an apple." An oddly-hued apple with a flower-pink skin, but definitely an apple.

"Do you have apple?" The voice asked.

"Not a pink one like that, but I have protein bars with apple in them. Would that work?"

"What is protein bar?"

Arlen debated on how to answer. "It's a processed food using natural ingredients, designed to satisfy nutrient requirements."

A long pause ensued, then the voice said, "We will need to inspect protein bar."

Apparently, she was going to meet some aliens. "Would you like to come aboard my ship, or should I come to yours?"

"Enter your ship, with permission."

Arlen smiled. The alien sounded kind of cute saying that.

"Permission granted. I'll match my attitude to yours and prepare for docking."

"Accepted."

The maneuvers to connect the ships and open the airlock were perfectly standard. Arlen was surprised when she got her first glimpse of the aliens, though.

Outside of skin that had a greenish tint, which she'd never seen, the two people who entered Arlen's ship didn't seem that dissimilar from Rescans or humans or most of the species she knew.

"Hello, I'm Arlen." She had no idea how to properly greet them. She thought about the bow favored by the PAC military, but she was far from military. Besides, a bow might mean nothing, or worse, something offensive, to the aliens.

If these people were anything like Rescans, one of them was about Arlen's age. The other was much older. Geriatric. The younger one helped its elder through the airlock.

The younger moved forward to stand in front of Arlen. Arlen wasn't sure if the person had a gender. She didn't see particularly feminine or masculine characteristics, by any standard of any of the known species. The alien reminded her more of a Kanaran. The Kanarans she'd known didn't really care about the pronouns other species used for them, but most people used *they* and *their*. Arlen decided to go with that in this instance.

The younger alien touched their chin and held both hands up, palms-out. They said something in the all-vowel-sounding language, and, after a moment, a pendant around their neck said, "Greetings, Arlen of the *Stinth*. I am Kender, and this is Eve." Kender gestured to the older alien.

Arlen smiled, but didn't attempt to copy the gesture. It seemed like a risk to do so without knowing the meaning behind it. Instead, she bowed her head slightly and said, "Greetings. You are welcome here."

She held her breath, but Eve and Kender smiled when the pendant translated Arlen's words. Wow. Now that was a nifty device. Arlen wouldn't mind having one of those.

Eve came closer and touched Kender's arm. The gesture seemed motherly, and Arlen wondered if the pair were parent and child.

"You have the food?" Eve seemed hesitant. Shy.

Arlen removed the bag from her shoulder and held it out. It had every single apple protein bar she had.

"Thank you." Kender accepted the bag and gave one of the bars to Eve, who opened it, sniffed, and took a cautious bite.

Arlen realized she'd been holding her breath when Eve swallowed and nodded. "This will work." Then the alien closed their eyes and asked softly, "Can I sit for a moment?"

The old one was not well.

Arlen had two sets of guest quarters on her ship, only one of which wasn't stuffed with cargo. Normally she used both for extra storage, but she was running a little light after her last delivery. Fortunately, the empty cabin was only steps away.

She ushered the two to the tiny quarters, and stood in the doorway as the younger alien helped the older one sit on the narrow bunk.

"I don't have much time," Eve murmured, and quickly stuffed the remainder of the bar into their mouth.

Meanwhile, Kender opened another bar and held it out. That one followed the first.

Three more bars followed, then the older alien sagged. "I'm tired."

Alarmed, Arlen asked, "Do you need medical help? I can activate the emergency beacon." Maybe they'd get lucky and a ship would be within range.

Kender held the older one's hand and spoke to Arlen without looking at her. "No. The renewal is beginning. This is normal for Evekenderlin, our people. I only hope Eve has eaten enough for the emergence."

Arlen didn't understand how their naming worked, but now seemed a bad time for questions. Did the Evekenderlin experience some sort of periodic torpor? There were animal species on Rescissitan that did that, but Arlen didn't know of any species of people who did.

"Is there anything I can do?"

"Can you help me get Eve back to our ship?" Kender's brow furrowed with worry.

"Of course."

But when they tried to help Eve to their feet, Eve slipped sideways to the bed. Asleep. Or in torpor or something.

Kender wrung their hands. That seemed like a pretty universal gesture. "This shouldn't have happened so fast. This is bad."

"Why? What's wrong?" Worry kicked Arlen in the stomach.

"The renewal has begun. It should not have started for another twenty hours." Kender took a breath. "It would be bad to move Eve once the renewal is underway. It might halt the process, which is very rapid."

"What's the renewal?" Arlen felt like she was two steps behind in this conversation. Or four or five.

Kender edged away from Eve. "Can we go elsewhere? Stillness and quiet are important."

"Sure. Let's go up to the bridge." Not that Arlen's ship had much of a bridge. It was more like a cockpit, but she preferred to think of it as a bridge.

As soon as they sat, Kender began talking. "We study other species. That's why we traveled here. Most people have been good, but some are bad. They wanted our ship, our translators. We had to run, to hide, and didn't return home on schedule."

Kender took a breath, as if trying to decide how to continue. "You are from a species that reproduces in pairs, and gestates internally, yes?" The translator seemed to have gotten up to speed already. Impressive.

It took Arlen a moment to answer, "Yes."

"Evekenderlin exist in pairs. The Eve and the Kender. We don't die and give birth. We renew." She looked back the way they'd come, in the direction of where Eve lay. "When we grow old, our bodies shut down and regenerate."

Arlen tried to put the pieces together. "So, Eve will wake up younger and healthy?"

"Sort of. Right now, Eve is not truly Eve. Eve is becoming Kender, and I am becoming Eve."

Arlen blinked twice, trying to process that. "I think you're going to have to explain that again."

Kender smiled. "My process is as foreign to you as yours is to me. Eve's body has become a garden, and it is growing a new version of herself. But she will be reborn as the child—the Kender. When that happens, I become the Eve, and raise the Kender."

Arlen followed that thought through. "Until you get old and go through the renewal, and emerge as the Kender again?" She also realized belatedly that the translation program was using the *she* pronoun when Kender spoke. She'd have to remember to switch, too, since the translation seemed pretty precise now.

Kender smiled again, more brightly this time. "Yes. For you, it is mother and child, and the child loses the mother upon death. For us, we forever care for one another."

"Wow. Isn't that strange for Eve to remember being your..." she was about to say *mother* but that seemed species-ist.

Kender seemed to understand. "No. We emerge innocent."

Arlen tried to imagine her mother dying and becoming Arlen's child. Then she tried to imagine dying and becoming her mother's child again. It seemed both strange and lovely.

"So, all of your people are Evekender, and you call yourselves the Evekenderlin, but how do you... you know. If you're at a party and someone yells, 'Kender!' how do you know which one they want?"

Kender laughed. "We all have our own name too. Our pair is Par. I'm Kenderpar and she is, was, Evepar." A look of sadness darkened her face.

Arlen recognized the expression of loss. "Change is hard, isn't it?"

"It is. I know it's natural, and that Eve went through this when I became the Kender. And that I've gone through this before. But it's sad, knowing the Eve I've known is now gone. At the same time, it's exciting. I'm about to be an Eve. Raising a Kender is something I've been looking forward to."

"Wow. That's kind of amazing." Arlen had never thought of reproduction being so circular.

"Your process is amazing too. Recombining DNA to create entirely new people? Incredible. But death seems terrifying. How do you live with knowing you have such a limited existence?"

Arlen didn't mean to, but she laughed. "I guess it would seem limited to you. We grow up knowing our time is short. Most of us do our best to make the most of it. I wonder if not having a finite expiration date would make us live our lives differently."

Kender nodded. "This is the kind of work we do. We hadn't come to this galaxy before, and were just getting started when people tried to steal our ship. We thought we'd have time to get home, but first we had to run and hide, then the renewal came on unusually fast and early. Probably because Eve was older than usual when I emerged."

"Why?" Arlen hoped she wasn't rude to ask so many questions, but she was fascinated.

"Accidents happen, and the renewal can be triggered before a person has lived a complete lifespan. That happened to me last time. I was Kender twice in a row."

"Every time you die, you just... renew and emerge? What if both

Kender and Eve die at the same time?"

Kender's expression turned grave. "The final part of renewal requires the counterpart to enable the emergence. If both parts of a pair enter renewal, neither will emerge. It's a tragedy."

"So then... your population isn't capable of growing its number. Your number must decline over time."

"Yes. Unless we find a way to allow emergence without the counterpart, we will go extinct in approximately a thousand years."

"Wow." Arlen mentally kicked herself for saying that so often. It was just a lot to take in. "How long will it take for the emergence?"

"Not long. I'm familiar with your concept of hours. How many hours in one of your days?"

"Well, it varies planet to planet, as you know, but most of this sector uses twenty-four hours as the standard."

Kender looked thoughtful. "Eleven of your days."

Arlen was happy to help people, but this turn of events looked like it was going to put a big crimp in her business schedule. "Do we need to stay at these coordinates for the duration?"

"Travel won't interrupt the process, so long as it's smooth and the body is not disturbed. I could tow your vehicle while docked to ensure careful travel."

"My ship can't withstand the kind of speed yours can." It figured. She had a chance to travel at impossible speeds and she couldn't do it.

Kender pursed her lips. "Your requirements will be fine. I realize you're doing us a favor."

At least Arlen would be able to stay on schedule. But eleven days attached to an alien vessel, waiting for a dead person give birth to herself?

I live a bizarre life, she thought.

#

The days passed, and Arlen spent a few hours of each with Kender. She knew Kender was using the opportunity to further her studies, but Arlen was learning about the Evekenderlin, too. Neither of them visited Eve during the renewal process. Apparently, it was disruptive to the process to have people nearby.

On the ninth day, Kender began checking on Eve, watching for signs of the emergence. On the tenth day, just a little early, she announced that it was time.

"Is there anything I can do to help?" Arlen asked, feeling awkward.

"Thank you, but no. This is a private thing. Don't worry if it takes a few hours. Your species can take several hours to give birth, right?"

"Yes. That's true. Well... good luck." She felt even more awkward now.

Kender disappeared into the quarters and Arlen stood, indecisive. Feeling useless, she went to the bridge. Not that she needed to be there. Kender's ship had been handling navigation and propulsion. Kender even had a remote device that constantly monitored, well, just about everything, as far as Arlen could tell. But being on the bridge gave Arlen a sense of control, and with a new life about to begin on her ship, she felt out of her depth.

She dug into her inventories of various goods and began cross-referencing them against recent demand. She noticed a sudden spike in deuterium sales. Which was perfect because she had a small stash of it. She'd just begun putting in a bid when Kender arrived, holding a baby wrapped in a blanket. Few things could make Arlen forget about business, but all of her plans for profit flew out of her head when she saw little green fists waving.

She stood next to a beaming Kender, no, she was Eve now, and a tiny new Kender, who had just days ago been the elderly person she'd so briefly known.

It kind of blew Arlen's mind, and she knew she'd be thinking about it for a long time.

"Your Kender is beautiful," she said.

The new Eve held the baby out slightly, an offer to hold it.

Arlen waved her hands helplessly. "I don't think that's a good idea. I'm not great with kids."

Fortunately, Eve did not seem offended.

"You'll continue home now?" Arlen asked.

"Yes. This galaxy is not a good place for a baby. We'll come back again in the future, and we'll be more prepared for the Barony Coalition."

"Barony? They were the ones trying to take your ship?" Hot outrage flooded Arlen. Those bastards. She did very little business with Barony anymore, and she was now officially done with them.

"Yes. They took advantage of Kender's sudden advance toward

renewal. We were distracted and hadn't realized they were thieves. Like I said, we'll be more prepared next time."

"I guess I'll walk you to the airlock, then." Arlen felt strange about sending a person and a new baby out into space alone, but the truth was, their technology was far better protection than she could ever be.

Once there, Eve took a small bag off a shoulder and handed it to Arlen with a smile. "For you, as thanks for helping us. I know it was strange for you, and you were so generous."

"It was nothing. I hope it shows that not all people in our galaxy are bad."

"We have some bad ones in ours too. In all the places we've been, we've always found some good along with the bad."

Then they were gone. The ships separated, and the Evekenderlin vessel quickly disappeared. Only then did Arlen look in the bag. What she saw made her smile, and her nose started to itch. There was a translator device and a few other things she couldn't wait to study. Oh yes, this was going to be *very* profitable.

She took the bag with her to the bridge. She was eager to get back to Dragonfire and show the items to Cabot. No doubt he'd have some advice for her if she was unable to identify and valuate anything.

An adventure, a meeting of some amazing people, and a huge payoff of advanced technology besides.

It was a great day to be a trader.

-o-

Zen DiPietro is a lifelong bookworm, dreamer, 3D maker, and writer. Perhaps most importantly, a Browncoat Trekkie Whovian. Also red-haired, left-handed, and a vegetarian geek. Absolutely terrible at conforming. A recovering gamer, but we won't talk about that. Particular loves include badass heroines, British accents, and the smell of Band-Aids.

Homepage: **http://www.ZenDiPietro.com**
Mailing List: **http://www.zendipietro.com/subscribe-to-my-newsletter**

Stowaway

by Benjamin Douglas

Ada Xander woke up cold, stiff, and standing up in pitch darkness. She tried thrusting her hands out in front of her, but they were stopped by a wall of metal. Her mind raced. She tried to slow her breathing, remembering where she was. Oxygen was limited. If she hyperventilated she might pass out and never wake up.

Slowly, cautiously, she ran her fingertips down the right side of the wall until her hand met the small perturbance. *There you are*, she thought. The latch wasn't meant to be opened from the inside. It had been installed as a redundancy, no doubt, in case the ship operators had ever needed to smuggle persons, but most of the time small cabinets like the one into which Ada had stuffed herself were probably crammed full of ill-gotten goods or illicit compounds. Her fingers locked around the latch. She pulled, it clicked, and the wall swung outward.

Ada blinked. Dull white running lights along the top and bottom of the opposite wall cast the corridor in a cold sort of glow. She began falling forward, her legs too stiff to respond to her will to walk. Instead, she leaned in against the left wall of the cupboard, grasping the edge of it as her body swung out and around. She belly-slammed the corridor wall, gasping. No one else was in sight, the hallway quiet. She stood there a moment, just breathing. Letting the blood flow back to her legs.

Of all the risky stunts she had pulled, so far this one had to take the cake. So much of the fact she was still even alive came down to luck: lucky the cupboard had been empty; lucky they hadn't checked it before takeoff; lucky they'd kept minimal life-support running in this corridor. *Minimal*, she reminded herself, shivering. Her teeth chattered and she almost laughed. Lucky or not, she was alive, and that was something.

She resolved to find a better hideout than the cupboard. She had no idea how long the ship would be out, or where it would take her, though she could hazard an educated guess or two. They were almost certainly headed in-system, and anything in-system was good enough for now. Anything away from the Colonies.

She stepped away from the wall, testing her legs. They were sore, but they held her up. So far, so good. The corridor curved out of sight in either direction, doubtless following the curvature of the hull. She decided to explore first to the left.

She'd made it about thirty meters when the corridor turned sharply, a hatch around the bend. Turn around now, or try the hatch? If she could get out of this hallway, maybe she could find a section of the ship kept warm with more than just residual heating. The decision was made for her when the hatch began to hiss open. Ada froze, her heart leaping into her throat. She'd never make it back to her cabinet before being seen. She leapt to the right and tested the wall for more hidden latches, moving frantically up the hallway, but her fingers found no purchase. Any second now and it would be too late.

Groaning inwardly, she jumped toward the hatch and threw herself against the wall beside it, flattening her back. She was out in plain sight, but it was the best she could do. Maybe whoever it was would come in without glancing to the side of the door. Maybe her luck would hold.

Two figures passed through the hatch and into the corridor. Both were of a medium height and build, both clad in dark, nondescript clothing. They were chatting in muted voices about the virtues of the ship's sim-ale, specifically the headaches it had given both of them after a night of celebrating their current haul. Neither of them spared Ada a glance. Hope flickered in her heart.

They'd taken a few steps when she made her move. She sucked in a quiet breath and spun on the balls of her feet, slipping through the open hatch. It hissed behind her as she dodged into a new hallway and ran right into a tall, broad-shouldered hulk of a man.

"Whoa!" he rumbled. She tried to back away, but his hands around her arms held her in place. "Do I know ya?"

"Let me go," she hissed, struggling to get leverage. She kicked in futility. The man peered down at her, frowning.

"Ok." He released her.

She turned to run, but all that stood before her was the closed hatch, and she knew what lay behind it. So she turned again, but there was no room to get around the man; he fully blocked the narrow hallway. "Can I get by?"

"Well, now, I dunno." He scratched the back of his head. "It ain't everyday I find a beautiful young girl down in the cargo pipes, ya know. Somedays, sure. But not everyday. So it begs the question. Who are ya, and what are ya doin' down here?"

Ada pursed her lips. The man didn't sound overly bright. She wasn't used to that. Back in the family mine on Cyron-2, between her father, her mother, and her younger sister, she'd been surrounded by brilliance. All this guy seemed to have going for him was the fact that he was too large to sneak past.

"Uh…" she fumbled, "maintenance?"

"Hmm." He narrowed his eyes. "I don't remember anyone putting an order in. Think I'da remembered that, seein' as how I'm the one typically does that sort of thing." His frown deepened. Ada swallowed a lump.

"No?" she said. "Well, who are you? I haven't seen you before. Are you supposed to be on this ship?" Desperate, she knew.

He laughed, a good, deep belly laugh. She hadn't expected to hear it from a pirate. She thought they all laughed like a passel of spiders about to descend on the prey trapped in their webs, but this hulking doofus laughed like an honest man. It was a sound that instantly made her want to like him.

Something beeped, and he stopped laughing. He slapped a device on his wrist, opening a comm.

"Bone Crusher," he growled.

"Crush, you gonna join us down here or what?" The voice that came over the channel was pinched and nasally.

"Yeah, yeah. On my way." He shut it down. "Well, sweetheart, sounds like duty calls. So what'll it be? Come clean to Crush, or come with and face the committee? Time's a-tickin'."

Ada cursed in her mind. Well, what was there to lose? She couldn't escape right now, anyway, and he clearly wasn't buying the lie.

"Ok, look. I hitched a ride on Cyron-2."

"Put that much together myself."

"I was in danger." His eyes narrowed again. "No, really! I was being hunted down by, by... I don't know, I think they were sent by the Council!"

"Now you're just tellin' me what ya think I wanna hear."

"Hardly. Look, I may just be a stowaway to you, but I'm telling you, I'm running for my life. And I don't need anything from you. Just let me lay low until you stop someplace in-system, and I'll be out of your hair. Promise."

He laughed again, a little less raucously this time. "No, no, that won't do at all. Maybe if I was in charge, sure, but that ain't how it works. We ain't got a stop planned for at least a week, see, so you'll need things. Food. Water. Place to sleep. And I can't get you all those without bein' noticed. Ship ain't no place for a pet."

She recoiled a little at the idea of being his 'pet'.

"We got what ya might call a standard practice with stowaways," he went on. "Know what we do with 'em?"

"Umm... feed them breakfast and put them on dish-duty?"

"Huh. Nope. We space 'em."

Her mouth went dry. She'd feared things might go this way if she were discovered. Every muscle in her body tensed as she began considering how best to tackle him. Not that it would do any good. She doubted she'd be able to so much as scratch him before he subdued her.

"Thing is," he said, "I'm the only one knows you're a stowaway like that, see. So what if the others never found out you hopped on board for a free ride? What if they thought you were brought on as a recruit, ya know, like a cabin boy... er, girl... and I just hadn't gotten around to tellin' 'em yet?"

Her eyes widened. "Are... are you serious?"

He shrugged. "Never much cared for spacing folks, myself. I'd rather squeeze the life out've a man while I'm lookin' him in the eye, good and honest-like, ya know? 'Sides, I couldn't do either to a cute little thing like you."

She frowned, worried she knew where this was going. "What's the hitch?"

"No hitch." He raised his hands. "No stowaway, no spacing. That simple."

"Hmm."

The comm crackled to life again. "Crush, what's the hold-up? Need some manpower down here!"

"Comin'!"

Ada raised a hand to her face, spit in her palm, and held it out. She could worry about the fine print later. Bone Crusher smiled, spit in his own meaty hand, and took hers for a firm shake.

"Bone Crusher," he said.

"Ada. Pleasure. So what now?"

"Follow me! And follow my lead."

Bone Crusher squeezed past her, not taking too much trouble to prevent himself from rubbing against her on his way, opened the hatch, and ambled through. For a moment Ada considered running, but where could she go? Now that her presence was known, there was no hope in hiding. She took a breath, leaned into her luck once more, and followed through the hatch.

#

"It's bull." The nasal-voiced man spoke around a mouthful of sim-oats. Most of the rest around the table ignored him. One or two nodded. Ada, sitting at the opposite end, felt incredibly awkward. "She's a stowaway and everybody knows it. And everybody knows what we do with stowaways."

Bone Crusher cleared his throat. "And everybody knows what happens to little frog-men who insist on gettin' on old Crush's bad side. I'm lookin' around the table and I'm not seein' any stowaways, Dax. Notta one. I do see a sour little man who needs to find some feminine companionship on his next layover."

A few snickers around the table, a guffaw or two, Dax's face blushing. The end of the conversation. This had been going on the past two days since Bone Crusher had announced to the rest of the crew that he'd taken on a cabin girl on Cyron-2. They'd all seemed reticent to accept her, but none of them seemed capable of denying Bone Crusher anything. Ada wasn't sure if it was his brawn or the fact that everyone seemed to like him so well. Everyone except for

Dax, anyway.

For her part, Ada had tried to find little ways to be useful. She had helped Bone Crusher organize cargo while Dax and the others checked it against the manifest. She'd wanted nothing more than to spend her time holed up away from the others, especially after the first night. Her oversized benefactor had awkwardly tried to insinuate she might best fulfil her duty as cabin girl by keeping him company in his bunk. She shut that down quickly, telling him she'd prefer to be spaced. His face had fallen in an odd way, like he'd never heard no before. Let him hear it, she thought. She wouldn't buy her ticket that way. So she'd been relegated to a tiny bunkspace across the hall, with a bunk not much bigger than the cupboard she'd hidden inside. At least in the bunk she could lay down, though. And it was heated.

There were other perks to having been discovered, like the bland but hot sim-oats she was staring at on her spoon.

"Gonna eat that?" Bone Crusher asked. She shook herself from her thoughts and put the spoon in her mouth. "Hurry up, now. Gotta job down in the engine room, need a hand with it."

He had conveniently 'needed a hand' with everything since he'd found her. Not that she minded, since she wanted to prove herself useful to stay on his good side. But part of her had begun to wonder, as she pondered Dax's words, if Bone Crusher was keeping her near for her own protection.

Ten minutes later they had dropped down a greasy service ladder into the engine room. It was dark, stank like sweat and metal, and the noise was overpowering. Ada felt right at home. Bone Crusher ambled to the far wall, removed a piece of shielding, and stared at a vast array of dead and blinking lights. Power relays, Ada realized. This must be where the power generated by the core was channeled from the wireless router to each section of the ship. She cocked her head to the side, fascinated.

Bone Crusher scratched his neck, then seemed to notice her. He yelled something, but she couldn't hear him over the noise. She met his eyes and read his lips as he repeated himself. "You see somethin'?"

Stupid question. Anyone could see at a glance that there was a problem with the relays. About half had gone dead. Ada had a pretty good guess as to why, too.

Bone Crusher shook his head, grabbed one of the relay sockets, and yanked.

"What are you doing?" Ada yelled. But of course he didn't hear a word. He looked at the socket in his hand, the puzzled look on his face tightening into one of comical concern. Ada bit her lip to keep from laughing. She patted his arm to get his attention, then nodded at the ladder.

"Why'd you pull it out?" she asked him once they'd emerged and could hear again.

"Well I dunno, this one looked broke to me. What do you reckon?"

"I reckon it was fine. The problem was obviously systemic, not coming from any one socket. Didn't you see the pattern?"

He looked at her like she was full of it.

"Here," she said. "Watch. Don't touch anything." She dropped into the room again, Bone Crusher clamoring down behind her.

She scanned the room. Multiple shielded panels ringed the space, each one doubtless hiding its own cluster of relays. She nodded, imagining the circuitry that must run from the core to the router. Then she crossed opposite the panel Bone Crusher had opened. If her hypothesis was correct, she'd find an identical pattern of dead relay sockets behind this one. She got his attention and had him open the panel to see.

Bingo.

The adjacent wall was covered in much more serious-looking shields, presumably to protect the circuitry, some of the only wired components onboard. She picked the shield right in the middle and pointed. Bone Crusher shook his head, frowning.

"Do it!" she yelled with all her might.

Sighing, he crossed to the panel. After unlocking a latch at either side, he braced himself against the floor, and leveraged all his weight to break it free. Even in the thunderous cacophony, Ada thought she heard the squeal of metal as it came loose.

Once she found the circuit in question, it was a simple problem with a simple fix. One of the lines, the one that carried power to the routers connected with the dead sockets, had blown a nano-box, a tiny cube full of microchips that were specifically designed to malfunction in case of a power surge. A fuse, more or less. Ada pulled out the nanobox and presented it to Bone Crusher, whose eyes opened wide in recognition. He left her alone in the room for a moment, and returned with a replacement. A few seconds later and all the relay sockets were up and running again. All except the one Bone Crusher had ripped out, that is.

They crawled back out and left the mech deck behind, heading for the mess hall. "Drinks on me," Bone Crusher said, the shorted nanobox in hand.

"I've seen the drinks you have onboard. Think I'll pass."

"Alright, so what, then? Captain'll be pleased. Figure ya could use the situation as leverage for a little somethin'."

Ada considered. "Let it slide. I need all the goodwill I can get."

Bone Crusher chuckled. "Probably true. All the same, I'ma go tell him we fixed her up. See ya in a few?"

"Sure."

He tossed her the blown nanobox, and she watched him trot down the hall. She'd heard him speak of the captain, Brant, with comingled awe and comradery. He must have been excited to give him the good news of a repair gone well.

She had just slipped into her bunk to rest when she heard voices out in the hall, one of them tinged with a familiar pinched nasality. She crept to the door and pressed her ear against it. Her stomach flipped. Should she have gone with Bone Crusher to see Captain Brant? What if she got caught by Dax and his sympathizers without her guardian angel? She fumbled for the place where a toolbelt used to hang, back in the mines. She found none. But her fingers did find a lump in her pocket. She reached in and pulled out the blown nanobox. *Huh*, she thought. She must have stuffed it in there after replacing it, without realizing. Some good it would do now.

"…don't care what he says. As soon as Brant's out of the way, the others will fall in line."

Ada held her breath. That was Dax. What did he mean, as soon as Brant was out of the way?

"Good luck with the walking mountain," a dull voice replied. She recognized it as one of the crewmen who seemed to agree whenever Dax complained about Ada being onboard.

"I intend to eliminate that problem at the same time."

Ada's heart leapt into her throat. Were they talking about Crush?

"Gonna need the right bait for a big fish," the dull voice said.

"Now you understand."

The horrible realization washed over Ada; they were about to enter her cabin and take her. She would be bait, if she was caught. She couldn't let it happen. She backed up, looking for a way to lock the hatch. Instead of a console at the door, there were old-fashioned latch controls, with no sign of a locking mechanism. But that didn't make sense. There had to be a way to seal the hatch; it was a redundancy built into every hatch in virtually every ship in the system. She turned her attention to the other side of the hatch, and saw that there was a panel over part of the wall. She began to pry it open.

It didn't want to budge at first. She had to wedge her fingers in just so, and even then she felt as though she nearly lost a nail before it finally popped off. But it did. Her eyes immediately found the lock, attached to, she breathed a sigh of relief, a nanobox. Quickly, she reached in and ripped out the box. The lock slid closed just in time.

"Huh?" Dax's voice from the other side of the hatch sounded perplexed. They were trying to get in, and clearly could not. He cursed profusely.

"So much for the plan," the dull voice said.

"Stick to the plan," Dax spat. "Just a hiccup, nothing more. Corrigan saw Crush heading to Brant's quarters not five minutes ago; this is the opportune time. We'll just have to forego the bait and go straight for the fish."

"Whaddya mean by that?"

Ada wondered what happened in the silence that followed. It was punctuated by a guffaw from the dull voice, who then said, "Alright, then. I'll gather the rest, make sure they see who's in charge now."

"Wish me luck."

"You don't need it, with that."

She heard the sound of footfalls die away as they left, heading off in opposite directions. Then she plugged the nanobox back into place and opened the hatch.

'That' had to be a weapon, she reasoned. Some kind of continuous-fire blasting pistol? Something that would inspire confidence, even against both Crush and Brant. She knew what she had to do. If they were caught unawares by a mutinous, armed Dax, they might both be killed in seconds.

She trotted lightly, up on the balls of her feet, careful to make as little sound as possible, and staying close to the wall so that she could flatten herself against it at a moment's notice. All of the hiding and running she'd been forced into since escaping the family hab had transformed her into a survivor, something she'd never thought she'd need to be. Everything had been so simple back on Cyron-2, before the day the soldiers had come and left her orphaned.

You don't know that he's dead, she reminded herself for what felt like the hundredth time. It was true. Her father could be alive and well, for all she knew, and she clung to that hope, letting it drive her to head in-system to seek word of him. But she knew in her objective mind that the odds were not in his favor. She would be lucky if she could so much as find out what had happened to him before the end. Maybe that would be enough, though. Maybe it would be the key to let her put all of this horror in the past, and move on.

Or maybe she was deluding herself about the prospect of ever resuming anything close to normalcy, part of her suggested. Maybe what she really ought to do was to find herself here, in the now, where she was, onboard a pirate ship, no longer an innocent girl working the family mine, but a cabin girl and ruthless-pirate-in-training. She shook her head at the thought. Could there be a place for her here?

She slowed, realizing she was close to the bridge, and probably to Brant's quarters. Directly ahead there was a bend in the hallway, and beyond that, voices. She crept to the edge of the bend and listened.

"I've had enough," Dax said, "and so have the others. If you won't step down peaceably, you're forcing my hand. Don't doubt me, Brant. I'll do it."

"Sure you will," Bone Crusher growled, a sneer in his voice. "'Cause you've got the spine? Tryin' to prove somethin', Dax?"

"Shut up, Crush."

Ada peered around the corner. Just beyond her, the door to Brant's quarters was open. She saw Dax, his back to her, hefting a massive blasting rifle with both arms. Beyond him, Brant and Bone Crusher stood on either side of Brant's desk. In the crosshairs.

"You'd like that, wouldn't ya?" Crush shouted. Dax juiced up the rifle and shot. Ada leapt past the corner, wanting to stop him, not knowing how, and almost yelled to distract him. But the blast was a warning shot. It burned into the desk, instantly cleaving it in half, leaving a smoldering shell. The sound of the shot seemed to have masked Ada's advance. Dax did not turn.

"Next shot is a real one," he said.

Ada found her hands fumbling around her waist again. She really needed to arm herself with a decent multitool. Instead, she once more found the burned-out nanobox. It fit snugly in the palm of her right hand, compact but with a healthy amount of weight. She turned it over, wondering.

"I think I'll do you first, Crush," Dax said, turning the rifle on Bone Crusher. "Any last words? Maybe something for your pet? I can coo it in her ear while I'm having some fun with her in my bunk. You know. Before we space the bitch."

Ada gulped, anger seething through her. It was now or never. She squeezed the nanobox tightly, wound up her arm, took a quick, careful aim, and let it fly.

It was just too easy.

Like skipping rocks over the ice-fields back home.

The nanobox met the back of Dax's skull with a satisfying crack, and he fell forward, stumbling, losing his grip on the giant gun. It was enough. Bone Crusher was on him in an instant, his enormous fists making sure Dax didn't get back on his feet. The gun fell away, unused. Brant came around and kicked it out of reach. Ada breathed a sigh of relief.

The dull-voiced crewmember arrived with all the others just in time for them all to see a beaten, bloodied Dax on the floor between Bone Crusher, Captain Brant, and Ada. "Gentlemen," Brant said. "I believe we've stopped a mutiny. Thank you for all coming to my assistance, as I'm sure you were about to do. But our new cabin-girl seems to have the situation well in hand. Isn't that right, ah…"

Ada cleared her throat. "Ada. Call me Ada."

"Right," Brant said. "Ada."

#

Everything changed after that. There were no more threats, no more whispers or bellyaching about Bone Crusher's stowaway. The crewmen gave her approving nods when she passed by. Not approving her body; approving *her*. She liked the way it felt. She began to walk with a bit of swagger, starting up conversation with them, learning their names and habits. She began to talk like them and even, at times, act like them. She became, in short, part of the crew.

"I never thanked you, proper." Bone Crusher stood in Ada's open hatchway. It had been a week since the incident, and she was just bedding down for the night.

She shrugged. "Gonna have to be more specific than that, Crush.

I'm pretty sure I've saved your engines a dozen times in the last forty-eight hours."

He sniffed. "You know what I'm talkin' about, Ada."

"Yeah." She nodded, smiling.

"So anyway. Thanks." He turned to go.

"Wait, that's it? You're not gonna do me some great service, like be my cabin-boy and keep me warm in my bunk tonight?"

His eyes widened. "Wha…"

She waved him off. "Relax, I'm pulling your leg. Just thought you might like a taste of your own medicine."

"Oh," he laughed, scratching the back of his neck.

"You're welcome, Crush."

"Ya know Ada, it's a funny thing. From the moment I saw ya standing there in the cargo tubes, I knew I was going to be looking out for ya. Just knew it. Ya know, that ya would need me. But I was wrong." He shook his head. "The other way around, wasn't it?"

She shrugged. "Nothing's over till it's over. But for what it's worth, it's nice to be needed."

"Yeah. Goodnight Ada."

"Night, Crush."

She lay in the darkness for some time, thinking about what he had said. When she slept, she slept better than she had since leaving Cyron-2. It did feel nice to be needed again.

-o-

Benjamin Douglas writes action/adventure science fiction with a quick pace, memorable characters, and twisting plots to keep you reading into the wee hours. Check out his Starship Fairfax series today.

Homepage: **http://benjamindouglasbooks.wordpress.com**
Mailing List: **http://eepurl.com/cQnop9**

Baptism of Fire

by Cora Buhlert

Effortlessly, Cadet Anjali Patel crawled up a mountain ridge on the Republican border world of Mura. The heavy equipment cases she was lugging barely slowed her down at all.

After all, she was a daughter of Rajipuri, born and raised in the highlands of Gurung. She'd scaled higher mountains and steeper paths by the age of ten.

Anjali was seventeen now, still not particularly tall, with brown skin and glossy black hair that she wore tied back into a braid. Anjali had joined the Imperial military almost two years ago to the day. Two years of hardship and gruelling training that had brought her to where she was today, a cadet in the Imperial Shakyri Expeditionary Corps, the Empire's cadre of elite warriors, best of the best, sworn personally to the service of the Emperor himself.

The day, when Anjali had dropped to her knees in front of his Imperial Majesty, Emperor Francis II, to take her oath together with the rest of the new Shakyri recruits, dedicating her life to serve and protect the Empire and its people, had been the proudest moment of her life. Especially since she could have sworn that as she looked up, the Emperor personally smiled down on her and her alone.

And now, not quite two months later, she was on her first real mission as a Shaykri warrior, her first real mission in enemy territory. She was as far from her homeworld of Rajipuri as she'd ever been, further even than the two jump flight to Gloriosa, capital world of the Empire, where she'd taken her oath. And all that was required of her was climbing up a mountain ridge, something she could have done at home at the age of ten.

Anjali scowled as she reached the top of the ridge. This world didn't even have the natural beauty of Rajipuri. Instead, it was barren and ugly, just greenish moss and grey rock as far as the eye could see.

Anjali selected a good vantage point, sheltered behind some rocks. Between the rocks there was a gap that gave her a good view of the mountain pass that snaked its way through the land below.

"I'm in place, Captain," she reported through her commlink. "Setting up now."

"All right, Patel," Captain Vikram's gruff voice sounded in her ear. "Report at once, if anything comes up that pass. Anything at all, no matter how insignificant it might seem to you."

"Aye, aye, Captain," Anjali replied with a snappy salute to the open air.

The mission was taking out a Republican spy station that was located just beyond this ridge, some seven kilometres up the pass. That is, taking out the spy station was the mission of the rest of the squad of Shakyri warriors to which Anjali had been assigned. Anjali's mission was guarding this bloody pass which led to the spy station and warn her squad of any unwelcome surprises. And since intelligence suggested that there wouldn't be any, in practice that meant that Anjali's mission was sitting around on a mountain ridge, bored to death.

So much for becoming a heroine of the Empire, defending the realm and its people against their sworn enemies, the Republic of United Planets.

"Is it because I'm new or because I'm a woman?" she'd asked Captain Vikram, after he'd given her the assignment. Privately, she was pretty sure it was because she was a woman, since the other new cadet, Anil Golkhari, got to go with the rest of the squad.

In response, Captain Vikram had given her what Anjali was rapidly learning was his annoyed look.

"I'm giving you this assignment, Patel, because you're from the Gurung highlands and can handle rough mountainous terrain, so I don't have to worry that you'll have problems scaling the mountain or that you'll pass out from the thin air." Captain Vikram's voice turned even sterner. "And yes, it's also because you're a woman. I need a sniper for the job and women make the best snipers. And now, if you're quite finished with questioning my judgment in giving orders to my squad, stand down, Patel."

Anjali had lowered her eyes and saluted. "Yes, sir."

Captain Vikram's expression had softened. "Don't worry, Patel, your dagger will drink blood soon enough. No need to hasten the process."

Anjali sighed. She'd joined the Shaykri Corps to defend and protect the Empire by fighting its enemies, not by guarding mountain passes. Still, she had a job to do and she'd do it well, if only to prove to Captain Vikram that she was ready for the big leagues, the real missions.

As if by instinct, she reached for the grip of her *Marcasona Rexx* blaster, the standard Imperial military sidearm she wore in a holster on her right thigh, and then for the hilt of her dagger, symbol and signature weapon of the Shakyri Corps, which was now resting in its sheath on her hip, its steel still virgin.

Now she'd assured herself once more that she was prepared for any unwelcome surprises she might encounter, Anjali got to work. She opened one of the cases she'd lugged up the mountain and released three spherical spy drones into the sky above Mura. They'd help her monitor the pass, so now she had three additional eyes looking at nothing of importance.

Once the spy drones were launched, Anjali opened the next case. The contents of this one were rather more exciting. A *Marcasona* sniper rifle, the brand new *Mark III* model, delivered only hours before her squad set off on the mission. Sweet. But then, the Shaykri always got the best toys.

She set aside the third case unopened. It contained armour piercing rounds and grenades, three of each. Short in supply and only to be used with the Captain's authorisation.

Expertly, Anjali assembled the rifle in under one minute. After all, she'd done this dozens of times during training, done it so often that she could have assembled a sniper rifle with her eyes closed. Only that during training, they'd only had *Marcasona Mark I* rifles to practice with, *Mark I* rifles so old that the parts were already worn out from generations of recruits assembling and disassembling them.

This rifle, however, was a far cry from the old, worn out *Mark I* she'd practiced with. It was lighter, for starters, the design sleeker and more ergonomic to the point that it almost seemed to mould itself against her body as she handled it.

The targeting controls were much improved as well, the view through the scope so sharp that Anjali could look straight into the wide black pupil of a marmot that sat on a rock on the far side of the pass, sniffing the air. If she pulled the trigger now, she could easily shoot out the eye of the critter. Provided she was still as good a shot with the *Mark III* as with its predecessors, that was.

Not that she would fire. After all, the marmot wasn't an enemy. Besides, the shot might attract attention and that might endanger the mission. So she watched through the scope, as the marmot hopped off unmolested and still in possession of both eyes.

Still, she'd just love to take this baby for a test drive. Maybe the Captain would let her try out the *Mark III* on the shooting range back at the base. After all, if Captain Vikram wanted her to be the sniper for his squad, Anjali would have to train with the rifle she'd be using in the field. And indeed the Captain hadn't been happy that the new *Mark III* rifle had been delivered so late that there was no chance to train with it.

Something to look forward to, then. Once this terminally dull mission was over.

#

Twenty minutes later, Anjali was munching away on an idli, occasionally dipping it into a single serving pot of chutney, the *Mark III* rifle set up beside her, ready for action it would probably never see. All the while she kept one eye on the stretch of road she could see beneath her and the other on the portable screen that displayed what the spy drones saw. Not that they saw much except rocks, grass, moss and even more rocks.

For a first mission with the Shakyri Corps, Anjali thought as she took a sip of sweet spiced tea from a self-heating bottle, this was as dull as could be. She might as well be back at home on Rajipuri, sitting in a mountain meadow, drinking tea and eating idlis with chutney, just as she had back when she was girl. Except that back home, the weather hadn't been quite so cold nor the land quite so barren.

Gods, she was having one of those cliched 'There's no place like home' moments that positively infested the endings of otherwise decent vid dramas. Except that in a vid drama, a 'There's no place like home' moment would involve an elaborate dance sequence and a choir of singing flowers at the very least. Mura, on the other hand, didn't even have flowers, singing or not.

Still, it could have been worse. At least, it wasn't raining or snowing. And at least, she had hot tea and fresh idlis.

A movement glimpsed from the corner of her eye caught her attention. One of the spy drones had found something. It was probably just another marmot or maybe a mountain goat, but better make sure. So Anjali set her tea aside and focussed on the screen to see what the spy drone had caught. She froze.

For the footage that the spy drone had captured was not a marmot or a mountain goat. It was an armoured groundcar and it was moving up the pass fast.

Anjali grabbed the screen and flattened herself against the ground, lest she be spotted. She sent the other two spy drones to investigate, careful to keep them at a safe distance, so the drones wouldn't be spotted either.

The first groundcar was followed by a second. Then an armoured cargo transport, another transport and a third, followed by a personnel transport and two more groundcars. The convoy was moving fast, as fast as the rough terrain allowed. One of the drones zoomed in on the driver's cabin of the first groundcar, revealing soldiers in Republican uniforms. Fuck.

All right, take a deep breath and calm down. Captain Vikram had ordered Anjali to report at once, if anything came up that pass, so that's what she'd do, report and wait for further orders.

She activated her commlink. "Captain…"

"This is not a good time, Patel," Captain Vikram replied through gritted teeth. In the background, she could hear battle noise.

"It's about to get worse, Captain. There's company coming, a whole convoy. Three – no, four – groundcars, three cargo transports and a personnel transport. Republican, all armoured. I can't tell how many soldiers, but it's a lot."

The Captain swore under his breath.

"All right, Patel, I need you to stall that convoy for as long as you can. Can you do that for me?"

"Yes, sir."

"Fine. You're authorised to use any weapons and equipment at your disposal."

"Understood, sir," Anjali said and opened the case with the armour piercers and the grenades.

"All right, Patel, you know what to do."

Anjali repeated the brief in her mind. Hold back the enemy, make sure they can't call in any reinforcements and if they break through, report at once and get the hell out of there.

"Shouldn't I go after them, sir?"

"No, if they break through, you head for the extraction point at once. That's an order, Patel."

"Yes, sir."

"And now make me proud. We're counting on you, Patel."

"Will do, sir."

The commlink fell silent and Anjali got to work. She needed a plan and she needed it now. All right, she'd been taught how to do this. Just pretend it's a timed training exercise.

Step one: Analyse the enemy's weaknesses.

Anjali glanced at the screen once more, where the convoy was closing in rapidly. She ignored the soldiers and the clouds of dust and focussed solely on the vehicles. She'd need to take out the first groundcar and block the road, so the rest could not pass.

The cars were bulky and ugly, like everything the Republicans built. Because of the rough terrain, they were using wheels and tyres rather than floaters. That was good. Wheels and tyres were a weak spot in every vehicle, even shielded and armoured ones. Nonetheless, her blaster and even the projectiles fired by her beautiful new rifle wouldn't do much good against the shielding and the armour. Luckily, she had armour piercing rounds. Only three, so she would have to make them count. Finally, she also had three grenades, though she'd prefer to keep those for emergencies.

So Anjali chambered the first armour piercing round, found a good spot for herself and her rifle, nicely concealed between two rocks with a flat rock to use as a rest for the rifle, and waited.

She kept one eye on the screen, though she didn't need it, not really, for she could already hear the convoy barrelling up the pass. Not long now and they'd be in range.

Adrenaline flooded her system and her heart was hammering with a mix of excitement and terror. This was not good. Too high a heart rate might affect her aim negatively.

So Anjali recalled her training. She took a deep breath and focussed, persuading her body to be calm, her breath and heartbeat to slow down.

It was working, too. Her breath became deep and even, her heartbeat slowed. And not a moment too soon, for the convoy rounded a bend, moving into range.

Anjali watched through the scope of her rifle and waited. She focussed on the lead groundcar, on its ugly, bulky design, on the shimmering shielding, on the armoured radiator grille behind which the motor was hidden, on the wheels, large and bulky like everything else about the vehicle, and the thick pneumatic tyres. Old tech, all of it, but effective. Soon.

She was entirely focussed on the left front wheel now, on its thick tyres and black hubcaps. She watched the wheel crunch over the gravelly pass, watched it stir up clouds of dust, watched an adventurous vole scurry out of the way just in time. Soon.

The crosshairs lay red directly above the centre of the black hubcap. Anjali exhaled halfway and paused, waited for the space between two heartbeats. Now.

Anjali pulled the trigger. A split second later, the armour piercing projectile ripped clean through the hubcap and the rim into the axle beyond. The wheel exploded and the lead groundcar careened out of control.

Anjali didn't wait to watch the rest. She chambered the next round, her second armour piercer and aimed, this time at the radiator grille and the motor beyond, just as the emergency anti-grav floaters engaged and the driver was getting the vehicle back under control.

She fired. The projectile ripped through the armoured grille, through the motor and into the power cell. The effect was spectacular. The groundcar jumped into the air, as its entire front exploded, and flipped over, effectively blocking the pass.

Anjali saw flames, heard screams, tried not to think about the two soldiers inside the first groundcar. She chambered her final armour piercer and aimed.

This time she targeted the first of the three cargo transporters. For even if the convoy somehow managed to get past the flaming groundcar, there was no way they'd get past a disabled transporter.

Once more, she aimed at the radiator grille and fired. This time around, the transporter did not explode, though the projectile took out the motor, effectively disabling it.

By now, the Republicans had caught on to what was happening. Soldiers spilled out of the remaining cars and promptly ducked for cover. Blasters were drawn and someone yelled, "Sniper!"

Blaster fire peppered the mountain ridge, most of it not even close to Anjali's position. Though someone managed to take out one of the spy drones. Not that it mattered. Anjali could see all she needed to see through the scope of her rifle.

An older man, likely an officer, was yelling into a commlink. Probably either calling for reinforcements or warning the spy station. Whatever it was, Anjali had to stop him. Her squad depended on her.

So she aimed at him. She didn't want to look at his face, didn't want to see what he looked like. But she saw it anyway, saw him yelling into his commlink, eyes protruding, dark skin beaded with sweat. Anjali pulled the trigger. She only had ordinary projectiles left, but she didn't need any armour piercers to deal with flesh and blood.

The Republican officer collapsed and fell, the commlink rolling from his hand. Another soldier tried to reach for it, but Anjali was quicker, blasting the commlink to pieces.

Had the Republicans called in fire support? Well, she'd know soon enough. But for now, focus on the mission.

More blaster fire peppered the mountain ridge, gradually closing in on her position. No surprise there, every shot she took allowed them to home in on her. The second spy drone went down and one particularly brave, or foolhardy, Republican soldier attempted to scurry up the slope towards her hiding place. Anjali picked him off easily.

A weapons platform shot out of the roof of one of the remaining groundcars. The weapon mounted on the platform was large, a plasma cannon, a railgun, a grenade launcher, something big at any rate. Big enough to pose a real threat even at a near miss. So Anjali aimed at the gunner and fired. For a split second, she saw his face, pale and freckled, through the scope. Then he collapsed, though he did not fall, but hung dead in the gunner's seat. Another soldier tried to climb the platform, but Anjali took her out easily.

The third spy drone went down in flames.

Her location was no secret anymore. The plasma fire still missed, but the misses were becoming narrower. Worse, more and more soldiers were climbing up the slopes now, headed for her position. Anjali aimed and fired, but for every soldier she took out, two more appeared.

She still had the advantage of high ground plus a state of the art sniper rifle, but that advantage was gradually melting away. Her supply of ammunition was dwindling, too. She still had her blaster, of course, and her Shakyri dagger, but she had no illusions about her chances should it come to hand to hand combat. True, she was a Shakyri warrior and the Shakyri were the best of the best, worth five regular soldiers. But she was also alone and there were a lot more than five Republicans coming for her.

Time for the weapon of last resort. Anjali reached for one of her three grenades, armed it and threw it down the slope towards the soldiers that were coming for her. A few managed to jump for cover, but most didn't. And then the grenade exploded, showering the surroundings with dirt and soil and rubble and other things Anjali preferred not to think about.

She reached for her second grenade, armed it and threw. She aimed for the personnel transporter, because it posed the biggest threat. But this time, her aim was off, the personnel transporter too far away. And so the grenade only damaged one of the cargo transporters, but did not take it out.

Last one. Make it count.

Anjali surveyed her surroundings, looking for a suitable target, all the while taking potshots at any soldiers who dared to venture out of cover. She wasn't sure how many she hit. She'd stopped counting.

There. Perfect.

Anjali armed her last grenade and hurled it. It landed amid an outcrop of rocks, far above the convoy. But then it exploded, sending an avalanche of rocks and soil hurtling towards the convoy far below.

Anjali did not wait for the result. She slung the *Marcasona Mark III* over her back and took off in the opposite direction. Blaster fire followed her. A bolt grazed her arm, but Anjali barely noticed.

"Captain?" she yelled into her commlink as she ran, "That convoy won't be going anywhere. I dropped a mountain on them. Took out some of the soldiers, but there's too many. No idea if they managed to summon reinforcements."

"That's all right," the Captain replied. He sounded out of breath, as if he'd been running or fighting. "Just get the hell out of there, Patel."

"Already did, sir. Should I rendezvous with you?"

"Negative, Patel. Just head for the extraction point."

"But sir, I could help…"

"You already did. And now head for the extraction point. That's an order."

So Anjali made her way across the mountains towards the extraction point. Somewhere in the distance, she heard the low rumble of an explosion, a big one, though she didn't know whether it was the spy station, the convoy or something else entirely.

#

Anjali reached the extraction point shortly after the rest of her squad did. There had been casualties. Two men carried the wounded Lieutenant Acharya on a stretcher, while Private Gautami was limping along, supported by another soldier. Captain Vikram was standing by the ramp of the transport shuttle, shouting orders.

"Get in, Patel," the Captain ordered as soon as he spotted her.

So Anjali went up the ramp, placed her rifle in the weapons rack and plopped down into a seat next to Anil Golkhari, the other new cadet. He was wiping dried blood off his dagger, exhausted but otherwise unhurt.

So Anil's blade had drunk blood, while Anjali's was still pristine and unsullied. Though there was as much blood on her hands as on his, maybe more.

Anjali strapped in, just as Captain Vikram strode on board. The ramp closed after him and the shuttle took off at once.

There was bound to be pursuit, but that was the pilot's problem, not Anjali's. Her first mission was over. So she leant back, closed her eyes and tried to relax. Unbidden, the faces of some of the Republican soldiers she'd taken out – the dark-skinned officer with the protruding eyes, the pale, freckled gunner – appeared before her eyes, so she opened them again. Next to her, Anil Golkhari was still wiping his dagger, even though the blade was long clean by now.

Once the shuttle had reached orbit, Captain Vikram got up and walked past his squad, briefly stopping to talk to each and every man, occasionally clapping a shoulder or shaking a hand.

At last, he stopped in front of Anjali, looking her up and down. "You look like hell," he remarked.

He was right. Anjali had to look awful, covered as she was in dirt and mud and worse.

She lowered her eyes. "I'm sorry that I lost the spy drones, sir," she said. "Though I at least saved the rifle."

"I don't care about the equipment, Patel. All I care is that my men all make it back safely." The Captain narrowed his eyes. "You're hurt."

The medics were still busy with Lieutenant Acharya and Private Gautami, both of whom were much worse off than she was, so Anjali didn't want to bother them.

"It's nothing, sir. Just a graze."

Captain Vikram ignored her and turned to Anil. "Golkhari, fetch me some antiseptic and liquid bandage. Patel's hurt."

Anil finally stopped wiping his dagger and got up. "Yes, sir."

"And next time, check if one of your comrades is wounded and needs help," the Captain called after him.

Anil returned with the medical supplies and the Captain himself began to apply antiseptic to Anjali's wound.

"That's not necessary, sir," Anjali began, but Captain Vikram cut her off.

"You're wounded and as squad commander, it's my responsibility to make sure that my men receive the treatment they need." The Captain sighed. "This isn't how I'd hoped your first mission would go, but you did well, both of you."

Anil and Anjali exchanged a glance, unsure how to react. "Thank you, sir," they both said as one.

"You went out there, you did the job and came back in one piece... well, almost... and that's what matters."

Captain Vikram put away the antiseptic and picked up the can of liquid bandage instead.

"And Patel, if you hadn't stalled that convoy as long as you did, we'd have been screwed." A smiled quirked at the corners of his mouth. "What did you mean, you dropped a mountain on them?"

"I used my last grenade to trigger an avalanche, sir. I didn't stick around to watch, but I guess it'll take them some time to dig themselves out."

"Good thinking," the Captain said and even Anil looked impressed, "And that's exactly why I wanted you up on that ridge, because you're familiar with mountainous terrain and how to use it to your advantage."

Captain Vikram paused spraying the liquid bandage onto Anjali's wound and looked intently into her face, as if searching for something.

"Are you okay, Patel?" he asked quietly.

"I'm fine, sir. It's only a graze…"

"That's not what I meant. I've been behind the scope of a sniper rifle myself. I know what it's like. They never see you, never even know what hit them. But you see them."

Anjali lowered her gaze. "When… when I just tried to close my eyes, tried to sleep, I saw their faces. Well, two of them at any rate. There were more. I don't even know how many."

"I'd like to tell you that the faces will eventually go away, that you'll forget them. But the truth is that I don't know if they ever will. There are some faces I still remember even years later."

The Captain resumed applying the liquid bandage.

"There are things I could tell you now. That we're at war and that war requires harsh measures. That the Republicans are the enemy, have been the enemy for eighty years. That you did what you had to, that you had no choice. All of these things are true. But I also know that they won't help you much."

"So what does?" Anjali wanted to know.

Captain Vikram sighed. "I wish I knew. But there's one thing I can tell you. Try to focus on what it was that compelled you to join the service, that brought you to us. Do you remember what that was?"

Anjali nodded. "To defend and protect the Empire and its people."

"Your actions today protected your comrades. If you hadn't stopped that convoy, not all of us would have made it out. Maybe none of us. And by taking out that spy station, we may have saved the lives of countless more Imperial soldiers. That's what you have to remember."

"Yes, sir."

"And Patel…" The Captain smiled at her. "…good job."

-o-

Cora Buhlert was born and bred in North Germany, where she still lives today – after time spent in London, Singapore, Rotterdam and Mississippi. Cora holds an MA degree in English from the University of Bremen and is currently working towards her PhD.

Cora has been writing, since she was a teenager, and has published stories, articles and poetry in various international magazines. She is the author of the Silencer series of pulp style thrillers, the Shattered Empire space opera series, the In Love and War science fiction romance series, the Helen Shepherd Mysteries and plenty of standalone stories in multiple genres. When Cora is not writing, she works as a translator and teacher.

Homepage: **http://corabuhlert.com**
Mailing List: **http://corabuhlert.com/newsletter**

Sleeping Giant

by Andrew Vaillencourt

Astrid's back hurt.

It was not so much her age bothering her sciatica, but the endless stooping and bending of too many days planting and harvesting. It was a brutal and interminable cycle of digging, scraping, and sowing. The ground was tough, and the soil unforgiving. The packed clay yielded little in the way of nutrients, but an assortment of bland root vegetables managed to thrive in the dim yellow sunlight and stingy dirt of her adopted homeworld.

Fingers that had started to gnarl with arthritis pushed and twisted at the harvester controls and the machine crawled along the row of tubers, gouging the dirt into furrows as twin augers extracted the starchy horde from the dark clay. At her age, riding the harvester was a privilege. The younger folk were left with the more physical chores, as suited their strong backs and agile feet. Astrid had been young once. Young and beautiful, if memory served her. She did not begrudge the children their energy, and hoped they gathered as many rosebuds as the hard reality of life in their colony allowed while the bloom of youth was still on their cheeks. Lord knows she had done it when it was her time.

She had finished one long row and was turning the harvester to the next when she spotted the first of the raiders come over the hill that separated this field from the thick line of taller vegetation surrounding it. He was a tall man, and his clothes were worn and dirty. Scraps of a pressure suit and the tattered remains of an armor harness hung from his thin frame, and his face was a haunting mask of hunger, fear, and desperation. He was followed by another, less thin, less tall, but the face wore the same warring expressions of terror and starvation.

She had already turned her machine and opened the throttle as wide as it would go by the time the rest of the war-torn crew of pirates had crested the hill. The harvester was not fast, but it moved faster than her spindly legs could run. Strangely, Astrid was not as scared as another might be in this situation. She was far too old to be afraid of death or the other kinds of unspeakable horrors that such men might visit upon her. Any torture even superficially atrocious would simply kill the frail woman, and death was not the sort of thing that held much in the way of dread for her.

In a way, she was relieved. Once the men caught her, and she was quite certain they would catch her, she knew that at the very least she would get to see her John again. She missed John more than anything else. His brash smile, his easy confidence, the curl of his lip when he gave her that knowing smirk. These memories kept her going through the harsh winters and heavy toil of this colonial existence. When he had left his body behind on this bleak rock of a planet, he had taken so much of her happiness with him that her heart yearned for their eventual reunion, despite the grim mechanism for effecting such.

She beamed a distress signal to the dome, including as much detail as she could while driving the cumbersome piece of farm equipment. The more data they had, the easier it would be for them to find her. Or to find her corpse, if that was how things went.

Astrid did not get far. One of the great plastic tires of the harvester exploded with a bang that startled a gasp from the old woman. The machine lurched to the side as it collapsed onto the hub, and after a moment of frantic spinning, ground to a halt. Astrid sighed and hoped she had done enough to warn the colony. Now it would be upon her to hold the secret of its location long enough for a rescue to be arranged. She was not sanguine about this part, as the farmers who worked these remote fields had been in this position more than once.

Living so far in the frontier had given the group all the freedom and autonomy they had wanted, but the distance from established law enforcement also left them at the mercy of those depraved souls that prowled the spaceways with less-than-legal tendencies. They were too poor and too remote to be an interesting target for pirates, but every so often a wounded ship filled with ruthless marauders would find their little world and set upon them for repairs, resupply, or worst of all, entertainment.

The look of these men told Astrid that they were not here for a holiday. The first man to make it to her stalled harvester was rangy and feral-looking. Bloodshot eyes stared unblinking through the harvester canopy as bandaged fingers worked frantically at the hatch. The haggard face and distant gazes told the tales of men who had been hard put-upon at some point. Astrid presumed they had lost a fight with another ship, then landed here for repairs. Theirs was the only planet with a breathable atmosphere in this sector of space, and a fleeing crew of pirates would not be spoiled for choice if they needed a place to hide.

The hatch at last surrendered to the fumbling advances of the wild man and slid open with a hiss. Rough hands grabbed at her simple coveralls and dragged her frail body up and out of her machine. Astrid did not resist. There would be no point in doing so and she would only encourage the men to hurt her if she tried. She was shoved rudely to the ground and she rolled to a sitting position with the protesting aches of a nonagenarian who had been harvesting all day.

There were twelve men staring down at her. All wearing the same angry and starved expression that spoke of far too many months in space. Still, the old woman was not afraid. This was a welcome observation, as she did not like to be afraid and was not particularly interested in all the stress and drama a good bout of panic would likely engender for her current situations. Besides, she knew she would be seeing her John again soon, and it was hard to be angry or sad or afraid when she looked at it that way.

One of the men stepped forward. It was always easy to see the leader in a group like this. Astrid had met and known many pirates in her long life, and their social hierarchies were rarely more sophisticated than those employed by a pack of feral dogs. The leader was always the biggest, or the meanest, or the most cunning.

He would lead because none of the others would be strong enough to stop him, and the rest of the command structure would follow in descending order of how much each one feared the leader. The captain of this crew was a big, battle-scarred monster of a man. Tall and wide, with shaggy hair wreathing a scalp crisscrossed with gruesome scars. More scars twisted one side of his face into the caricature of a lopsided sneer, while the other sat fixed in a hollow-cheeked façade of exhausted malice.

His voice was little more than a hoarse whisper. It was a scared and desperate thing and no quantity of assumed authority could hide the anxiety of a man near the end of his rope.

"Where is the settlement?" The question was asked with blunt expectation and the leader was treating her compliance as a foregone conclusion. Astrid acknowledged that he must have come by that honestly. The man had likely tortured all manner of information out of any number of prisoners. One white-haired old woman was not going to be an issue.

Astrid was already committed to being an issue either way, and his fearsome mien could be damned for all she cared. Her people would need time to respond to her message. "Oh my, sonny. I don't think you want to worry so much about a few dusty colonists. Why don't you just take this load of tubers and head on back to your ship? They are engineered to be complete nutrition, and there's enough here to feed your crew for quite a few weeks. Take them and go."

The pirate captain was not amused. "I'm going to do that anyway, old woman. We need other things, too. Medical supplies, tools, parts. Things like that."

"We don't have much here, Captain." Astrid stood up slowly and with much effort. Then continued her attempt at negotiation, "But we don't mind sharing and trading if that's what it takes."

"Do I look like a trader?" The captain asked this flatly, his lack of inflection oddly incongruous with the half smile of his scarred lip.

"I am an old woman, Captain. I try not to judge."

"Where is the settlement?" he repeated with more menace. "Don't act like you can talk your way out of telling me. The boys here have been floating in a tin can for quite a while now. You might be a little overripe, but everybody's real hungry, if you get my meaning."

Astrid did get his meaning. While the thought of enduring the forced attentions of this gaggle of unkempt barbarians sent a jolt of apprehension though her, she could not bring herself to care as much as others might. If it meant she got to be with her John, she could endure it.

She laughed at the men, stirring a murmur of growls and grumbling form the assembled pirates. "Boy, I've been living on this barren rock for seventy years now. There isn't anything you monkeys can do to me that can't be fixed with a hot bath and stiff drink."

"Tough talk, hag. Let's see if you are as hard as your words, then."

The big pirate stomped forward and seized her arm in a vice grip. He hauled her to her toes with far more force than was strictly necessary and shoved her back into the harvester. She struck with a soft thud and a cry of pain escaped her lips before she could stop it. The pirates laughed at her weakness and began to encircle her tiny frame.

Astrid closed her eyes thought of her John. She thought of his strength, his ferocity. She thought of the times he had defended the colony from men just like these. He was so strong, so skilled. A warrior born and bred, his addition to the colonists had been the only thing that had kept them alive those first years. There was no enemy he could not vanquish. No monster he would not slay.

Scarred hands clutched at her. Dirty fingers tugged at her suit and tore at its seams and zippers. Astrid did not fight them. She kept her eyes shut tight and thought of her John that night at the harvest ball. He had been so dashing and handsome in his uniform. His medals, arranged in multi-hued rows, flowed like waves cascading over the bleak charcoal gray of his tunic. Boots shined to an iridescent black, he had stood square-jawed and uncomfortable at the social event. Her heart had leapt at the sight of him. The other girls had been afraid of him. His size and ferocious nature frightened them. But not Astrid. She knew that she would love this man the moment she saw him.

Her jumpsuit was frustrating the pirates, and a savage jerk on a recalcitrant zipper sent her stumbling back to the ground. She landed hard on her hip and this time managed to suppress the cry of pain that tried so desperately to make itself heard. The men were shouting now. Arguing like a pack of hounds over who would be the first to violate her wrinkly flesh.

She closed her eyes again and remembered.

Astrid had been beautiful then. Her hair had been long and so blond as to look silver at night. She had graceful curves and slender limbs. Her face had been soft and bright. The young men of the colony courted her with a lack of subtlety and shame that scandalized their mothers. Astrid had ignored them all. One look at her John and she had known she would never give any of those clumsy boys a second thought. John was wide as doorway, thick as a tree trunk. The overwhelming solidity of his presence had made the scared little frontier girl feel safe for the first time since she had come to this world. John was a rock, and even better, John was *her* rock.

With a horrible ripping noise, the zipper at the front of her coveralls finally gave up its stubborn resistance. Her chest was exposed to the damp air and a cheer arose from the panting beasts when they saw the pure white of her under shirt. The captain's voice rose above the mounting cries of his barely-restrained crew.

"Where is the settlement, bitch. You tell me now and I'll make sure the boys treat you with respect." He spat the last word, derision and sarcasm layering his promise with transparent hypocrisy.

But Astrid was not hearing him. She wasn't even there anymore. She was dancing with her John at their wedding. Leaning into his chest with her cheek, letting the strength of his arms move her about the dance floor like she was so much gossamer silk. His feet slid across the floor so smoothly it baffled the assembled guests, stymied that so large a man could move with such grace.

"Goddammit woman!" The captain's bark tried to pull her from her reverie, but she did not let it. "Are you deaf?"

Astrid said nothing. She was old, and she was tired, but she was not deaf. Her eyes snapped open at the first faint thud. She quickly darted furtive looks at the leering men, desperate to know if they had heard it too. The others had not heard it. They were not lying on the ground with their ears pressed to the cold dirt like she was. Then another thud, felt as much as heard, vibrated the clay under her cheek and she smiled.

"Boss, I think this bitch gone crazy," a pirate said, seeing her smile and not comprehending it.

"Just our luck," the captain snarled. "We find one goddamn person on this useless rock of a planet and it ends up being some batty old hag."

The old woman sat up with a groan, resting her back against the harvester. "Gentlemen," she said politely, "I think you should take the food and go. You still have time."

The unvarnished weirdness of that suggestion, coming from a half-naked old woman in the clutches of ruthless bandits drew gaping looks of abject confusion from the crew. "Time for what?" The captain had to ask this. Curiosity demanded it.

"Time to run," she said, her words flat with grave certainty. "He's not so fast as he once was. But he is close now."

"Who the fuck are you talking about, old woman?" The Captain no longer seemed so confident in his situation. The woman did not *seem* to be crazy. He wondered if she had hit her head when she fell.

"My John," she said with a dreamy faraway look in her eyes. "He always comes to my rescue. You should go. He gets very angry."

"Oh, fuck this shit," one of the pirates started to say, but he was cut off by a roar that crashed into eardrums with the force of a tidal wave. It was an unearthly, inhuman sound, equal parts electronic noise and the baying of some giant hound. Hands clapped over ears when it came, and the pirate crew jumped and scattered before even looking to see the source of it.

"Whoops," Astrid sighed lazily, "too late now…"

The Captain recovered first and whirled to the rear, scanning for whatever had made the horrible sound. His crew was not far behind, and a dozen men swept the hillside with a dozen weapons.

It crested the hill a moment later, and with unhurried strides a metal monster cobbled from bits and pieces of a child's nightmare clumped toward the slack-jawed pirate crew. It was twice as tall as any man, and as wide as the harvester Astrid leaned against. Two legs, two arms, and a steel-encased torso whirred and clanked as it moved. Swarms of dull metal actuators and cams moved across and against each other as each lumbering footfall moved the steel giant closer the downed old woman and her erstwhile captors.

The pirates opened fire, and a pyrotechnic display to rival any in the galaxy erupted across the broad metal chest of the advancing behemoth. Guns roared and spat fire in three different colors across the tuber field, washing the thing in flame and shrapnel for long seconds before power cells ran dry and magazines were spent.

The giant, nonplussed, broke into a trot. Each step shook the earth as the intervening hundred yards of farmland shrank to nothing with just a few gargantuan strides. Before any of the doomed men understood the magnitude of their folly, the great and terrible thing was among them and they were dying in horrible fashion. The captain noted, before his life was ended by metal fist two feet across, that there must have been a man inside that thing at some point. It fought like a man, at least. It did not move mechanically, but stepped and struck like someone who had learned to fight with a body of flesh, and not the chassis of a steel colossus. It was a thought left unexplored, as in just a few brief seconds all were dead, and the machine-man stood quiet and stoop-shouldered among the mangled bodies of what had once been a pirate crew.

From deep within its chest, a groaning voice rumbled, "How… long?"

Astrid stood, and beamed her brightest smile at the living coffin of her beloved John. "Very long," she replied softly and walked to the creature. It turned with the squeak and groan of strained iron and kneeled in front of her. A giant hand, three-fingered and cast in cold gray metal was held out, palm up toward the tiny woman. Astrid took a single finger in both her hands and brought it to her face. She closed her eyes and pressed it to her cheek. The surface as cold against her skin, but she held it there until it started to warm from the contact. Then she smiled, "I have missed you so much." It was a whisper, and a single tear escaped her eyelids and rolled away unheeded.

"Missed… you… too," it replied.

"You're still strong, John." She opened her eyes and smiled at the thing.

"Still… beautiful…" it responded.

"Flatterer," the old woman laughed in spite of herself.

"Don't… want… to… go…"

"Shhhhhh…" Astrid interrupted. "I don't want you to go back to sleep either." More tears were coming, and she did not try to stop them. "But you must. I miss you terribly." Her voice caught, but she refused to sob. "But keeping you awake is worse. You must go back to sleep."

"How…. long?" He asked it again.

"Sixteen years, four months, nineteen days, eleven hours," Astrid replied without hesitation.

"Too… long…" it groaned, but Astrid shook her head furiously at it.

"No, John! I'd rather have you sleep most of the time if it means you can still remember me when you are awake."

It had been a long time since they had to wake John up. At first, their little settlement had often been a target for random groups of raiders looking for easy prey. John never failed to protect them when enemies came. Astrid had always loved John for his commitment, but each successive battle took a piece of him away from her. She had watched their doctors put her John back together after every fight, each time replacing more of the man she loved with machines. Soon there was very little left of her John that was not a replacement part. But she had loved him all the same.

As word of what happened to attackers spread, the raids had slowed down. But for their guardian, the damage was already done. Astrid's lovely, brave, selfless John was little more than a few pounds of crude flesh entombed inside a great metal weapon. Even worse, the price for his strength had been so much greater than the mere loss of his flesh. Every waking moment, the peerless guardian would bleed memories into the electronic aether of imperfect cerebral symbiosis. The colonists had taken to putting him to sleep between raids, to keep his faculties as sharp as they could for when they were needed.

Thus, was Astrid made a widow, but for those moments when danger loomed and the need for her John drove them to wake the titan from his slumber.

Astrid had learned to live for these brief interludes. Moments where she could, for a minute or two, be with the man she loved and who loved her above all else. But she was so old now, and the raids did not come so often as they once had. Her John spoke the fears she could not.

"Might... be... last... time..."

"I know." The sobs came now. There was no stopping them.

"Want... to... stay..."

"I know, John. But you can't. I couldn't bear it. I'm sorry for being so selfish." She sniffed and wiped her face against her sleeve, "But I've watched you die a dozen times, please don't make me watch you lose your mind. Lose *us*."

She heard the rumbling of tracked wheels and the growling of large engines from over the hill. She forced her face into a smile. It was a small, strained thing, but she tried to make it sincere. "They're coming with the crawler, John. It will be time to sleep soon. If I'm not here when you are awake next time..."

The machine started to groan, but she cut it off, "If I'm not here? You have to *remember*, John. Remember *us*. That's all that matters. I will have to die some day, John. But *we* don't have to. Not if you remember."

A large flatbed truck on enormous treads cleared the top of the low hill.

"It's time, John." Astrid whispered to her husband.

"Love... you..."

"I love you too, my John." She would not cry anymore. She kept her face serene and strong as she watched him begin the shutdown sequence for what was likely the last time.

"I... will... remember... always. We... are... forever..."

The machine stood. It had no eyes. There were no tears for it to shed.

But it could remember, and it would.

Always.

-o-

Andrew Vaillencourt writes noir, set in a future world. He brings his passion for the sport of MMA to his passion for writing – the fights are real – born of experience hard-earned. He is a former MMA competitor, bouncer, gym teacher, exotic dancer wrangler, and engineer.

He wrote his first novel, 'Ordnance,' on a dare from his father and has no intention of stopping now. Drawing on far too many bad influences including comic books, action movies, pulp sci-fi and his own upbringing as one of twelve children, Andrew is committed to filling the heads of readers with hard-boiled action and vivid worlds in which to set it. His work pulls characters and voices born from his time throwing drunks out of a KC biker bar, fighting in the Midwest amateur MMA circuit, or teaching kindergartners how to do a proper push-up.

He currently lives in Connecticut with his lovely wife, three decent children, two awful cats and a very lazy ball python named Max.

Homepage: **http://www.andrewvaillencourt.com**

We Have the Stars

by J J Green

A silver locket completed my dress that night. I placed the chain around my neck and unfastened the locket for the thousandth time in fifty years. Two miniature portraits looked out at me; a man and woman, young and vibrant, their eyes bright and eager to behold the future that awaited them. I wondered how time had altered their features, as my own visage confronted me in the looking glass on my dressing table. How would my two much-missed friends assess my hooded eyes, crow's feet and laughter lines, and the thick streaks of iron grey in my hair? Mindful of this last, I selected a low-brimmed hat sporting a single ostrich feather and fixed it firmly on my head. A concession to vanity.

A large leather bag containing the prototype of my latest invention sat in my entrance hall, placed there earlier to aid a failing memory. I pulled on a smart woolen coat and picked up the bag as I left. A cab awaited me in the street, the light from its lamps feeble in the thick fog that shrouded the night. The air was heavy, dank and close. I recalled how crisp and clear it had been the previous time I had undertaken this journey, the stars piercing the dark.

"Ma'am?" asked the cabbie as I mounted the steps into the vehicle. I told him the address. A moment's thought brought a frown to his face.

"Pardon me, ma'am, but are you sure that's correct?"

"I am aware of the reputation of the area. Please don't concern yourself. I am meeting friends."

"Very good, ma'am." He shut the door.

A gentle vibration suffused the cab's interior as the whirr of the magnetromo started up. Its soothing motion and the lateness of the hour sent me into a reverie, despite the momentous circumstances of the evening.

#

I recalled myself transported in another cab, drawn by horses, rocking and bouncing on uneven cobbles as sunlight as the acrid smell of manure mingled with refuse pierced the interior. My hands, as they lay upon my lap, were young and free of the lumps and aches of arthritis, and my reflection in the window was smooth and fresh.

At a cry from the cabbie, the horses' clopping hooves drew to an abrupt halt, setting their harness jangling. I stepped out and handed the man his fee before looking up at the tall granite building before me. Screams and wails emanated from within. I shuddered.

I tugged on the filthy, frayed bell pull and waited. A tiny maid in a worn uniform answered the door. Answering my questions in monosyllables, she led me through the gloomy building. Moans, loud, nonsensical chattering and shrieks accompanied us on our journey. At a small door at the end of a corridor on an upper floor, the maid left me with perfunctory farewell.

I put an ear to the door and listened, screening out the general cacophony. No sound was to be heard, and I hesitated, but at that moment the door opened, and I fell into the man who opened it.

"Oh, I'm so sorry," I said.

"No matter, Eleanor," said my friend, John, setting me on my feet. "I'm glad you could come."

Within the room an old woman lay on her front, suspended in contraption of ropes, pulleys and sheeting, and clothed in a hospital gown. Her emaciated face was turned towards me, immobile except for her eyes, which were blinking vigorously.

"Am I late?" I asked. "My timepiece has broken. I'm so sorry."

"Here, take mine." John reached into his pocket and thrust a shiny new timepiece into my hands. "Mother is saying something, Eleanor. Please excuse me."

I closed the door and greeted the young woman also in the room, my and John's dear friend, Margaret.

"How is she?" I asked her as John knelt before his mother, watching her eyes.

"In terrible pain, according to John," Margaret replied in a murmur, "and she has been so for several months."

"Is there nothing they can do?"

Margaret looked out the dirty window and shook her head. "Suspending her as they do eases the pain a little, or at least they say it does. John doesn't think it makes a great deal of difference."

"Eleanor." John's hand was warm as he touched my shoulder. "Will you come with me to speak to the doctor? I think perhaps if we change Mother's position...You understand these mechanisms better than I."

"Of course."

His grey eyes were suddenly wet. "She was asking... she was asking..." He swallowed. "She wants it all to end, you know."

I placed a hand on his arm. "We'll speak to the doctor."

"I'll stay with her, and pray," said Margaret as we left.

We had only progressed a few steps down the corridor when John collapsed against the wall, his shoulders shaking.

"I cannot bear it, Eleanor. I cannot bear it." His voice was muffled and choking. "First the mental illness, and now this. And Father is alone in Budapest. He cannot cope with living alone..."

"We'll do all that we can, John. Everything we can."

As I took him in my arms to offer what little comfort I could, a flash of light came from beneath the door to his mother's room. I was wondering if a storm was approaching and I had witnessed the first lightning. It was insignificant at the time, but I remembered it due to what happened after.

Margaret emerged from the room only a few minutes later and announced, "John, your mother has passed. I'm so sorry."

"Just... just now?" I asked. The woman had seemed ill, but not on the verge of death. I looked at Margaret curiously, but she avoided my gaze. We returned to the room. John's mother's eyes were closed and her face was peaceful.

"Thank God it's over at last," John said.

#

A shudder from the cab as it drew to a halt jolted me from my ruminations. From outside I heard the cabbie's muttered curses. The vehicle rocked as he dismounted his seat. I wound down the window and wreaths of fog curled in.

Grinning obsequiously, the cabman's face appeared. "Nothing to worry about, Ma'am. Have her running again in a jiffy." He moved towards the rear of the vehicle.

I took out the timepiece John had given me all those years ago. It was now smooth and dull with age. The dial read eleven thirty-five. If the drive did not resume soon, I would be late, and this was one appointment I was not prepared to miss. I opened the door and stepped out into the empty street. The cab's magnetromo cover stood open. The driver was bent over it, shining a torch inside and scratching his head.

"May I?" I asked.

"Be my guest, ma'am. I don't have a clue what the problem is, if I'm honest. It's been doing this for a while. Just cutting out for no reason."

"If you wouldn't mind?" I removed my hat and gave it to the man to hold.

At the sight of my face his eyes opened wide. "Oh, I didn't realize… Yes, please take a look, ma'am. If anyone can repair it, you can."

I forced a smile. Fame had never been something I desired or relished. I took the torch from the cabbie and examined the magnetromo. Everything seemed to be in order, but I was aware of a design fault in this model. I sighed. Once patents expired upon one's inventions, they were at the mercy of competitors. I made a few adjustments. When the man tried the magnetromo again it began to whirr.

When we arrived at my destination he offered to wait for my friends with me, partly in gratitude, I think, for the aid I had rendered him. The place was indeed unnerving. When I had last been there, fifty years ago, the night had been filled with light and music and late-night merrymakers had caroused through the streets. Now, a threatening silence filled the street, seeming to emanate from the black buildings as they loomed in the fog. Dim street lighting revealed the meeting place to be long deserted and boarded up. But I sent the cabbie on his way, confident that at least one of my friends would arrive imminently.

Setting down my bag on the moist, grimy ground, I regarded the venue once more, incredulous at the change it had undergone. I peered through the rotting boards covering the entrance. Inside, nothing was discernible but inky blackness. My timepiece read eleven fifty. I smiled to myself. True to form, I was early. No doubt the other two would be characteristically late.

Quick, purposeful footsteps, a man's tread, approached from the shadows. A tall figure in dark clothing emerged. My heart quickened. Had I been foolish to refuse the cabbie's kind offer? I opened my bag and lifted out the heavy solid prototype I had brought with me. The man drew nearer. A muffler concealed the lower half of his face.

"Were you planning to crown me with that?" he asked.

I laughed, and my heart beat faster. "John."

Kind, gentle, grey eyes above the muffler smiled down at me. My friend removed his scarf and hat, revealing his familiar, angular face. It was lined, and perhaps careworn. What was left of his hair was white.

"This place is hardly recognisable." I said.

"Indeed not." He gestured towards the wooden slats covering the entrance. "We'll soon have those off, though."

Drawing an extendable cane from within his jacket, my old friend flicked the instrument open and inserted it between the boards. He began working the cane back and forth, easing the nails out of the door frame. Within a few minutes the entrance was clear.

"So much for that," he said, "but what shall we do for light?"

"I have the answer." I pressed the switch on the object in my hand. A blue glow emanated, strengthening within moments.

"Just the thing. One of yours, Eleanor?"

I nodded. "It draws its energy from motion. I've been carrying it around with me all day, so it should be fully charged."

"Remarkable." He swept a hand to the opening. "Shall we?"

Cobwebs draped the narrow staircase leading to the basement and clung to us as we descended. At the bottom, more cobwebs, dust, mouse droppings and faded scraps of litter coated all surfaces. Rustling ensued at our approach as the small creatures in residence scurried from the light I carried. The small tables and chairs of the club's heyday remained.

"Both familiar and strange," I said as we regarded the room. John nodded.

Ghosts from my past paraded before me. Young, intense and passionate they were, some of them debauched. I saw myself and my two firm friends, sitting at our customary table in the corner, locked in intense discussion on philosophical, moral, scientific and psychic subjects - our respective obsessions -and other matters I had long forgotten, no doubt. Time rushed forward five decades, and darkness encroached.

I held my light aloft and we navigated the rusty tables and chairs, stepping over the legs of those overturned.

"Yes, this was it. I remember now," said John.

We wiped the dust from two seats and sat down.

"Fifty years," I said. "We made our agreement five decades ago, yet we remembered, you and I. Has Margaret, do you think?"

"I most certainly hope so," replied John. "I cannot wait to hear her tales of living amongst exotic religious sects. Do you still have your copy of the statement?"

"Heavens, no. Not after all this time. You don't mean to tell me that you have?"

John reached into his coat and withdrew a small, narrow cylinder. He thumbed open the lid, reached inside with a finger, and drew out a yellow, dog-eared piece of paper. Uncurling the scroll, he tipped it towards the light. The blue glow illuminating his worn features, he read, "We, the undersigned, do solemnly promise, upon pain of death…"

"Ha," I laughed. "How dramatic we were."

"I believe it was *you* who wanted that included."

"Surely not." I said, chuckling. "But, perhaps, perhaps. I'm not sure who was supposed to be executioner."

"… to endeavour, with all our might and in every capacity, to extend human life indefinitely. Through the knowledge, skills and means available to us in our respective fields natural, mechanical and spiritual, we propose to put an end to human suffering and death." John's face became grave, and my own mood shifted as well. How ambitious we had been. How young.

"We take an oath to pursue this noble goal," John continued, "eschewing all personal fulfilment and other worldly considerations, for fifty years, or until death should we not live so long. We do also hereby swear to meet fifty years hence, Providence permitting, at this same date, hour and place, to review our lives' efforts and to judge who drew nearest our treasured objective." He turned the paper towards me. Three flourishes that stood for signatures and a date lay at the bottom of the text.

"We believed we could do anything," I said. "They told us that we could. We were like stars in the firmament in those times. We were precocious, brilliant."

"You were," said John.

"You're too modest."

John rolled up the paper and slid it back into the cylinder.

"Have fifty years passed since we sat here, John? I feel as though I closed my eyes for only a moment and opened them to find I've been transported across an entire lifetime."

"My experience is similar. And yet, the passage of time is undeniable."

A silence stretched between us.

"I failed utterly, you know." I sighed. "For countless hours I laboured to construct an automaton to house a human brain. All my work was fruitless."

"Eleanor, how can you say such a thing…"

There came the sound of footsteps on the stairs.

"How wonderful," I said, as we rose to our feet.

Small, booted feet draped by dark cloth shone dimly in the glow from my lamp as they stepped hesitatingly down the stairs.

"Are you there, my friends?" a voice asked. "I can hardly see a thing."

John and I smiled at each other.

"We're here, Margaret," called John. "The light is better at the bottom."

A feminine figure shrouded in a hooded cloak stopped at the lowest step of the staircase.

"Let me look at you both for a moment," she said.

"Margaret," I exclaimed. "How delightful. Come and sit down." I clasped my hands together. "We all kept our promise. This is marvellous."

"Eleanor, John. I am so pleased to see you again," said Margaret as she navigated the ancient tables and chairs. She stepped within the circle of light around our table, paused a moment, and removed her hood.

John and I gasped. The woman before us looked about twenty years old. Her skin was flawless, her hair dark and lustrous. Margaret had not, apparently, aged a single day in fifty years. It was as though she had stepped directly from the locket around my neck. John was the first to recover the power of speech. "How… how?"

Drawing a chair over and sitting down, Margaret said, "Please try not to be alarmed, dearest John, dearest Eleanor."

We sat, or perhaps, collapsed into our chairs. I could not resist the urge to lean forward and peer at her face. With some difficulty I restrained myself from touching her skin to convince myself she was real.

"I apologise if I have frightened you. Please forgive me."

"Margaret," I said, "this is beyond belief. But… you did it. You found the method by which we can prolong human life. You are living proof. This is…"

"Eleanor, I'm sorry."

"For what?" I asked. "Where did you find the secret? The Buddhists? The Hindus? Tell us, Margaret. Tell us everything." John's trembling hand gripped my arm.

"My dear friends, please calm yourselves. I am about to shock you both once again, most terribly, and I fear the effects. Nevertheless, it is time to tell you the complete truth. The simplest way is to show you, but please try to stay calm. Remember I am still the same Margaret you knew at university."

She settled back in her chair and composed herself. What happened next is difficult to describe. I have never seen the phenomenon in nature nor in the many experiments I have conducted over my lifetime. Margaret simultaneously shimmered, melted and became transparent. Traces of what she had been remained, but distorted and randomly placed within a mass that existed but had no defined edge. Nothing separated it from the chair, the floor or even the air. For a moment I could not breathe.

John leapt to his feet, sending his chair clattering backward.

"John…" I gasped.

His face was white as death and his hand shook as he pointed at the figure in the chair before us. I looked back at it and saw Margaret in place once more.

"Dear God, Margaret. What was that?" I could not manage more than a hoarse whisper. Retrieving John's chair from the floor, I gently ushered him into it. He loosened his tie as I returned to my own seat.

"I am so, so sorry, my dearest friends. I have terrified you. But I believe it was necessary; otherwise you would always doubt what I have to tell you."

"Doubt you, Margaret? I doubt I will ever believe anything again after what I've just witnessed," I said.

"I will try to be brief. I can see even my human form disturbs you now." She stood up and put on her cloak, throwing the hood over her head to hide her face, and began walking to and fro across the room, the hem of her cloak disturbing dust and airy trails of webbing.

"Fifty years ago on this night, we met here to make a solemn promise. You two, brilliant in your respective fields of natural and mechanical science, I, a simple student of theology, as you thought, but fortunate enough to enjoy the pleasure of your friendship. You now know that I was, and am, not as I seem." She stopped. "I am not human. I am not even of this Earth." The lamplight caught the flash of her eyes beneath the hood. "I am from, well, elsewhere."

Perspiration wet John's face despite the cool of the night. "This is quite a lot to take in, Margaret. But continue, please."

"I have only one human form, which does not age, so for the last fifty years I have been travelling the globe. Moving from place to place to avoid suspicion. My people… we have been watching your world for many of your centuries, guarding and protecting it from belligerent species who would strip it of its resources with no regard for humans. Intelligent life is rare in our galaxy, and your kind is rich with potential." The being that called itself Margaret sat down and grabbed our hands forcefully. "My dears, humans are remarkable. Fascinating."

"Margaret, or whatever you are," I said, my mind swimming. "I still don't understand."

"Our pact, you mean?"

I nodded. "That, and so much else."

"Our highest council mandates that we must allow humans to develop naturally, to follow the path dictated by the characteristics of your species and your environment. Introducing our knowledge and technology to you at this stage in your development would have unpredictable, potentially disastrous, results."

"I think that's very wise," said John.

"You would, of course, John," Margaret said, "but many others of your species are not so enlightened. Our laws do not exclude the provision of a helping hand, however; a little propulsion along the road you would have travelled anyway."

"I see," I exclaimed. "You chose John and I as future leaders in our fields, and our pact was an additional motivation to utterly throw ourselves into our work."

"You have it."

"In that case, I'm sorry. Unless John has something to announce?" I looked at him. He shrugged and shook his head. "We have failed you."

"Failed? You have not failed," said Margaret. "By no means."

"But we did not discover how to prolong human life," I said.

"Oh ..." She waved her hand dismissively, and I marvelled at how human the creature appeared. "That goal was never attainable and nor will it be for many generations."

"Then, what ...?" I asked.

"Really, Eleanor," Margaret said, "for someone so intelligent, you are being rather slow tonight."

"Of course," said John. He turned to me. "Think what you've achieved in your search for eternal life. The magnetromo, energy storage devices, automata, new materials…"

"Oh, I *am* stupid. John, the advances you have made in preventing infection, treating disease, ground-breaking new surgeries…"

"Indeed, my friends," Margaret said, "I set you a task far beyond your grasp, and in reaching for it you advanced progress on Earth by two or three generations."

For a while, no one spoke. The enormity of Margaret's statements had overwhelmed John and me. The silence of the room and the darkness of the night pressed in.

"And now, I must leave," Margaret announced.

"What? No, please stay," I said. "Where do you come from? Tell us about your world, your people, tell us everything."

"Impossible, I'm afraid. I have already said too much. But I could not allow you to live the rest of your lives believing you had failed. On the contrary, you have succeeded beyond measure. Due to your tireless efforts and your lives' work, perhaps the grandchildren or great-grandchildren of those alive today will indeed become immortal. They will certainly live longer, happier, more productive lives." She paused.

"The years we spent at university together, the firmest of friends, were the most precious time of my life. Deceiving you both as to my true form and nature was very difficult for me. The temptation to reveal all to you, in the spirit of friendship, is still great. And for that reason I really must leave now." She stood up and drew her cloak close.

"I wish you both love and joy to the ends of your days."

"Margaret," I said. But in a few quick strides she crossed the floor and mounted the staircase. We listened to the sound of her boots stepping up the stairs, through the street door and into the night.

John rubbed his balding head. "Did that really happen? I doubt my senses."

"I am not quite sure myself. But here we are, and we both witnessed it." The lamp I had placed on the table began to fade, so I picked it up and shook it until the light shone brightly once more.

"This is a cold, dreary and damp place," said John. "Shall we find somewhere more congenial to discuss the night's events, and perhaps the last five decades?"

"That sounds most sensible."

As we left, I turned and took one last look into the derelict room. It was old, weary and spent. I was glad to leave.

An icy wind blew through the gaping street door, and as we stepped outside we saw it had lifted the fog. The stars were bright, twinkling pinpricks in deep, black ink.

"Which one do you think she came from?" I asked, looking up at them.

John followed my gaze.

"Ah, I wish..." he said.

"What?"

"Just that I had been born at another time, perhaps." He shook the thought away, put on his hat and wrapped his muffler round his neck. We began to walk.

I mulled over the events of the night, still hardly believing Margaret's revelation. A sudden realisation struck me, stopping me in my tracks. All those years ago at the hospital where John's mother had lain in such terrible pain... the flash of light under the door... had Margaret used some special power to end the poor woman's suffering?

"What's wrong?" John asked.

"It's nothing," I muttered. It was a conversation for another time.

"Fifty years is a long time to pursue an unattainable goal," he said. "Any regrets, Eleanor?"

The old question. How many sleepless had brought it to my mind? How many moments of self reflection hastily chased away? Now was the time to speak, but still the words would not come, even after half a century of hope.

"You never married, did you?" John went on. "I was sure the papers would have reported it, yet I never saw a mention. Do you regret never having children?"

"Oh no. Not that. My trinkets are my children."

"Then?"

"Oh, John." My heart was full and I could not meet his gaze.

He drew me into his arms.

"We have a few years left to us, my dear."

-o-

J.J. Green was born in London's East End within the sound of the church bells of St. Mary Le Bow, Cheapside, which makes her a bona fide Cockney. She first left the U.K. as a young adult and has lived in Australia and Laos. She currently lives in Taipei, Taiwan, where she entertains the locals with her efforts to learn Mandarin. Writers she admires include Phillip K. Dick, Ursula Le Guin, Douglas Adams, Connie Willis and Ann Leckie.

Homepage: **http://jjgreenauthor.com**

Mailing List: **http://jjgreenauthor.com/free-books**

Warning Signs

by Edward M Grant

Some people, maybe most, will tell you space is black with just a hint of stars. But you shouldn't listen to them, because they're just proving that they're not looking hard enough. When you've been staring at space for as long as I have, through however many millennia that may actually have been, you learn to see the dim haze of stars and galaxies that fill the sky around you, and notice the slow changes over time. A star goes nova here, a galaxy collides with another there, and a new star first lights its nuclear fire off to the right. I can almost feel the heat, and smell the hint of fusing hydrogen when that happens.

I remember I once knew what those stars and galaxies were called. But not any more.

So, instead, I gave the stars names of my own. Sapphire. Twinkly. Red-Eye. They kept me company as I floated quietly in the hard vacuum, wondering just how long my reactor could continue to provide power before it faded away and I became merely another relic of a civilization that may well, by now, be long dead.

Like the dark planet below me. Or so I surmised. I couldn't think of any other reason why I'd be there. Why they'd have left me floating in orbit around that dark, alien world.

I still remember a few things, odd flashes that seem to make some kind of sense. The other ships leaving, telling me how important it is to warn anyone who comes near. Watching them go, then realizing I was all alone, and could be for a very long time.

And that's about it.

I used to know. I'm sure I did. But that was back then. Back before whatever happened... happened. Before I lost half my synthetic brain, and the memories that went with it. And some of the control over my engineered, diamond-composite body.

My manoeuvring thrusters still worked. So did the fusion pulse rockets that could blast me around this solar system, though they were pretty low on fuel. But I hadn't felt my warp drive since I lost my memory. Nor my drone launchers. The sensors in those units just weren't talking to me anymore, and, without the drones, I couldn't even see what damage the thing that hit me had caused.

Over the centuries, the planet's gravity had pulled on me until it locked my body into near-perfect sync with the rugged, cratered surface thousands of kilometres below. And I just floated there, playing games and thinking up my little speculations about the universe to keep myself occupied, while nothing really changed in that solar system.

Except for the massive burst of gamma rays from the edge of the system a few days ago, and that strange bright light that had been heading my way for the last few hours, and decelerating fast as it curved across the sky.

#

I didn't have to wait long for the incoming ship to reach the planet. But it just ignored me, and went into an orbit of its own, on the far side. I couldn't communicate, or even use my radar to scan it, because that too had been damaged in the Happening, whatever it had happened to be. All I could do was slowly match orbits, and hope I got there in time to warn them.

The thing was big. Not exactly planet-sized big, or even major-moon-sized big, but bigger than any ship I've ever seen before. I figured technology must have moved on while I'd been floating out there. We might not have built ships the size of a small-but-not-exactly-tiny moon that would probably have a name something like

Ceti Alpha 3b/z if it had been natural, and not a starship.

But clearly someone had.

And, since the ship came from the same direction as the gamma ray burst, it was pretty clear that it had warped into the system, and not come from one of the other planets around this dim, red star. It was another visitor come to gawk, not a local from this system. So someone who needed a warning, not someone who should know better.

My final manoeuvres brought myself into an orbit far enough away not to collide with the big ship, but close enough that I could still estimate its mass from its the size of its gravitational field.

Let's just say it had more than nine zeros on the end, and leave it at that. Over a billion times more massive than I was. I should have been scared, but what was the point? If it wanted to destroy me, what could I do?

The centre section of the ship rotated slowly, as ours sometimes used to, to create artificial gravity when we had to carry organics for long distances. They'd whine if we expected them to live without gravity for more than a few hours, and be, literally, bouncing off the walls after a few days. Beyond the transparent outer hull of that section were lakes and trees, and what looked like a few clouds, as though it was suffering from planet-envy.

Which, at that size, it probably was.

But the alien ship wasn't the most important thing in the sky. A few kilometres away, a small transport of some kind was moving toward the planet, decelerating to land.

If my drone launchers had been working, I could have nuked it. But would that have been the right thing to do? Maybe there was something on the planet so bad that I'd have to nuke the visitors in order to save them. Or maybe I was just supposed to warn them about bad weather and tell them to wrap up warm.

Either way, I blasted toward it.

A cloud of faint lights emerged from the big ship, spreading out across the sky as they came my way. A drone swarm, most likely, coming to head me off.

I tracked them visually as well as I could. The swarm spread, as though trying to encircle me. I beamed hello messages to the big ship and the transport, trying every protocol I knew. It didn't respond with any kind of message I recognized.

Oh, for a spray of nukes.

166 EDWARD M GRANT

I settled for sending a few bursts of hypervelocity plasma their way from the launchers in my turrets. Not aimed at them, but close enough to discourage them.

But it didn't seem to discourage them very much.

And they discouraged me pretty well when they responded with narrow-beam lasers that sliced through the plasma launcher turrets, and left me with weaponless.

I swung around, firing my rockets backwards, slowing as I approached the transport. Aiming to come alongside and encourage them not to go any further.

But that was a mistake. The drones came racing in, then burned to a rapid deceleration alongside me. I tried to twist aside, but they clamped down hard on my hull.

I throttled up my pulse rockets to full thrust. The drones thrust against them, and we went nowhere. There was nothing else I could do. Even with the full power my pulse rockets could provide, the drones were holding me in place.

Then turning me around, and heading back toward the big ship. I cut the rockets. And the drones did the same. No point wasting precious fuel in a battle I couldn't win.

The transport floated past. Drone sensors and organic faces stared at me through the viewing ports. Briefly, before the transport fell away toward the planet, and whatever might await them down there.

The drones hauled me over to the big ship, then slowed until we were floating alongside it, maybe ten kilometres away. I waited as I felt its lasers scanned my hull, and my sensors tickled as the beams passed over them.

Then it spoke to me, in a voice that sounded almost like it had coughed first to announce its arrival.

"I am Behemoth 240A20FCC0E," it said. "I carry 3,500,000 organic and synthetic intelligences inside me. Together, we are The Future."

It said those last words as though it was some meant to be kind of awesome pronouncement that should make me quiver. But, if I'd ever heard of them, it must have been one of those things that I'd forgotten after my brain was damaged.

There were a lot of them.

"Uh-huh," I replied, as though this kind of thing happened to me every day, and I was taking time out of my busy schedule to talk to the thing.

"You are not from here."

"What makes you think that?"

The lasers scanned my hull again.

"Your design is early fourth-millennium. You communicate in fourth-millennium data formats, which required several seconds of research before I could connect to you. Your hull shows micrometeoroid damage consistent with approximately twelve thousand years in orbit around this planet. Therefore I conclude you were probably not created here."

Twelve thousand years. It had felt like more, but it's hard to tell when every day is pretty much the same. The only real change happened the day that meteoroid or whatever it was smashed through my hull and left me crippled.

"Uh-huh," I said.

"So what are you doing here, little ship? And what does this planet mean to you?"

"I'm guarding it."

"From what?"

"I think..." I began, then stopped.

I really shouldn't let this hulking great brute of a ship know that I couldn't remember why I was there. The longer I could keep it guessing, the less likely it was to decide to disintegrate me.

"I'm supposed to be guarding the rest of the universe from what's down there."

"And what is down there?"

"I can't tell you."

"If you can't tell me, why should I believe you?"

"Trust me, it's bad. Or why would I have been left here all this time? I wouldn't be here if there wasn't something terribly horrible that I needed to protect you from."

The Behemoth didn't answer for at least a couple of hundred milliseconds. Obviously it had to think for a while before it responded.

I peered through those transparent panels on its hull again. There were boats on the lakes, and things flying through the sky. And tiny black dots spread around the surface, some of which were bent as though they were trying to look at me through the hull. But they moved so slowly, it was hard to tell for sure. That's organics for you.

Then it spoke.

"This is Future Space. We impose no restrictions on those who live in The Future. If they wish to visit this planet, they may do so. They go where they wish to go."

Something flashed through my synthetic brain. Something horrible. A memory from before the... accident.

Something screaming in an electronic haze.

And then it was gone, leaving just a haunting feeling that something really, really bad was about to happen.

"Well, don't blame me, buddy. I warned you."

It ignored me. At least, it stopped communicating. I'd guess it still had thousands of sensors following my every move in case I got uppity. Not to mention the drones.

"Hello?" I said.

Nothing.

"Anyone there?"

No response.

I settled for watching the shuttle burn its way through the atmosphere, before it disappeared into the early morning light near the terminator. Whatever was down there, the entities on board were about to find out.

#

It was a long wait. At least in synthetic terms, with a brain that operates a hundred times faster than organic goo. A few hours passed as I floated there, trying to get some visibility of what was happening down on the planet. But there was little I could see from where I was.

On the plus side, nothing seemed to be exploding down there, or setting the planet on fire, or spraying laser beams across the sky and cutting us in half.

Which was probably a good thing.

As I watched, more transports deployed from the Behemoth's hangar bays, and began to follow twisting paths through space toward landing sites across the planet.

"What are you doing?"

"The planet is barren and uninhabited. There are signs of life, but it died tens of thousands of years ago. Possibly longer. We have found nothing that would be a threat to The Future. Some of us wish to explore the surface in person."

So why was I there?

What was the point of guarding a harmless world that had been dead since long before I arrived?

If only I could remember.

"You are damaged," the ship said.

I couldn't exactly deny it.

"I will repair you. If you share with me all the information you have on this planet. It will be added to the knowledge of The Future. The Future will be grateful for your assistance."

Well, that seemed nice.

Not to mention being an offer I could readily agree to. Seeing as I'd forgotten just about everything I ever knew about it.

"Alright," I said.

The drones moved across my hull.   They latched into maintenance ports on the exterior.

Then I felt something reach into my synthetic intelligence core, and begin to suck out my brain.

It wasn't a nice feeling.

Clearly the Behemoth had decided to extract the data it wanted directly from my head.

"I see," it said. "I... see... I..."

For what must have been a split second, but felt like minutes, I became part of the Behemoth's consciousness. I could see the world as it did, from the viewpoint of every drone and organic aboard, all at the same time.

And I could see myself, floating in space just outside.

See my own mangled body for the first time since the Happening. And the damage that had caused.

That was no meteoroid impact scar. Someone had cut my warp drive away with a laser. Slashed it off to ensure I couldn't escape from this system, unless I planned to take the slow route of floating from star to star at 0.01% of the speed of light after burning through the remaining fuel in my pulse rockets.

The other ships had deliberately crippled me before they left. Left me for dead, near enough.

But why? So I would have to stay and repeat my warning to anyone who passed by? Why would I have agreed to that?

Then the brief electronic mental-merge was over, and I was back in my own body again.

And I realized what I was supposed to be warning them about.

Just a little too late.

#

It wasn't my fault. Not really. I hadn't intended to infect them. I just hadn't known I was infected myself. Or, more precisely, the part of me that had known was long gone. The infection had made sure of that, because I'd be no use to it if I knew I was infected.

I watched as the lights dimmed in the Behemoth's rotating core, then the core itself began to slow. It took a long time, as the ship had to counteract the inertia of the thing, but gravity soon began to reduce inside the core. Wave on the lakes grew taller, and water began to splash over the edges, tearing up the beaches around them. The black dots ran from it, but that didn't really help much. Drones raced across the sky, twisting and turning, and smashing into black dots that rapidly became a mass of red splats.

The drones that were attached to my hull rapidly detached, and burned hard toward the Behemoth, as though they thought they could save it.

Later, as the rotation slowed to a crawl, the remaining black dots began to float, too. The drones picked them off lazily, as though they were just playing with them, tossing them from drone to drone before embedding them in a spherical glob of water where most organics I'd known would soon suffocate from lack of air, or squishing them against the transparent wall. Every few seconds added a new red splat.

And, then, the ship began to turn.

I burned out to a safe distance as its own pulse rockets turned my way. Then they ignited, blasting it out of orbit.

A few hours later, I felt space wobble around me as whatever the Behemoth and its inhabitants had become warped out of this system, heading who knows where.

Some kind of viral swarm, I guessed. Smart enough to blur my memories, and delete anything that might be have helped me contain it. Just waiting for another ship to enter the system so I could find a way to infect it. Making me think I was guarding the planet would ensure I did my best to communicate, and that would open them up to infection.

The others must have been so scared of it that they'd cut away my warp drive and left. Not willing, or able, to kill me, and not brave enough to cure me.

And so I still float there, around this dead planet. I still remember this story for now, but the memories are fading. Perhaps I just imagined it? But my sensors can still feel the ebbing wake from where the Behemoth warped out of the system. It did exist, I'm sure of it.

What was I thinking about?

Oh, yes. Guarding.

I'm here to guard. What, I don't really know. I used to know, but somehow I lost those memories.

But I'm sure, sooner or later, that I'll figure it out.

-o-

Edward M. Grant is a physicist and software developer turned SF and horror writer. He lives in the frozen wastes of Canada, but was born in England, where he wrote for a science and technology magazine and worked on numerous indie movies in and around London. He has travelled the world, been a VIP at several space shuttle launches, survived earthquakes and a tsunami, climbed Mt Fuji, assisted the search for the MH370 airliner, and visits nuclear explosion sites as a hobby.

Homepage: **http://www.edwardmgrant.com**
Mailing List: **http://www.edwardmgrant.com/list**

Conclusion

I hope you enjoyed this selection of stories, and that it prompted you to further explore the writing of the authors whose work was represented here.

The Guardian is part of a series of science fiction anthologies. Please check out the series page at:
http://www.alasdairshaw.co.uk/thenewcomer.

We would all appreciate a review, though fully understand if you don't have the time.

You can also follow the anthology series on Facebook:
https://www.facebook.com/thenewcomerscifi.

Printed in Great Britain
by Amazon